W9-BAY-278

GRIMMS' FAIRY TALES

WITH ILLUSTRATIONS BY ARTHUR RACKHAM

HERITAGE
EGMONT

This edition published 2013 by Egmont UK Limited
The Yellow Building, 1 Nicholas Road, London W11 4AN
www.egmont.co.uk

ISBN 978 1 4052 6738 0

1 3 5 7 9 10 8 6 4 2

A CIP catalogue record for this title is available from the British Library

Printed and bound in Singapore

55070/1

Foreword

Between 1806 and 1814, in the Hesse area of Germany, the Brothers Grimm collected together many strange and dark tales from ancient folklore. These included such classics as Snow White, Rumpelstiltskin and The Twelve Dancing Princesses, as well as the lesser-known gem The Goosegirl, a variant of the Cinderella story. The collection was first published in two volumes under the title *Kinder und Hausmärchen* (Children's and Household Tales) in 1812 and 1814. The first English publication dates back to 1823, and the translation in this edition, by Mrs Edgar Lucas, sticks faithfully to the original German.

In this volume you will also find animal tales such as The Bremen Town Musicians, adventure stories like The Valiant Tailor and Tom Thumb, as well as the irreverent account of a simpleton who is thrown out by his father, but ends up becoming the pope!

This edition of these famous tales includes illustrations by renowned artist Arthur Rackham. Born in London in 1867, he was one of twelve children and the son of a civil servant in the Admiralty Court. As a child he showed a real talent for drawing, and whilst training as a clerk in the Westminster Fire Office he also studied part-time at the Lambeth School of Art.

It was his illustrations for *Grimm's Fairy Tales* that truly set Arthur Rackham's career alight and he continued to refine them, adding colour and subtle variances, until the 1909 edition. He went on to illustrate *Rip Van Winkle* (1905), *Peter Pan in Kensington Gardens* (1906) and *Alice in Wonderland* (1907), as well as many other titles including *Fairy Tales from Many Lands* (1916) which is also published in an Egmont Heritage edition. His art won him gold medals in Milan (1906) and Barcelona (1911). Today Rackham prints and originals are valuable collector's items.

Contents

I

Snowdrop

It was the middle of winter, and the snowflakes were falling from the sky like feathers. Now, a queen sat sewing at a window framed in black ebony, and as she sewed she looked out upon the snow. Suddenly she pricked her finger and three drops of blood fell on to the snow. And the red looked so lovely on the white that she thought to herself: *If only I had a child as white as snow and as red as blood, and as black as the wood of the window frame!* Soon after, she had a daughter, whose hair was black as ebony, while her cheeks were red as blood, and her skin as white as snow; so she was called Snowdrop. But when the child was born the Queen died. A year after, the King took another wife. She was a handsome woman, but proud and overbearing, and could not endure that anyone should surpass her in beauty. She had a magic looking glass, and when she stood before it and looked at herself she used to say:

Mirror, Mirror on the wall,
Who is fairest of us all?

Then the Glass answered:

Queen, thou'rt fairest of them all.

Then she was content, for she knew that the Looking Glass spoke the truth.

But Snowdrop grew up and became more and more beautiful, so that when she was seven years old she was as beautiful as the day, and far surpassed the Queen. Once, when she asked her Glass:

Mirror, Mirror on the wall,
Who is fairest of us all?

It answered:

Queen, thou art fairest here, I hold,
But Snowdrop is fairer a thousandfold.

Then the Queen was horror-struck, and turned green and yellow with jealousy. From the hour that she saw Snowdrop her heart sank, and she hated the little girl.

The pride and envy of her heart grew like a weed, so that she had

no rest day nor night. At last she called a Huntsman, and said: 'Take the child out into the wood; I will not set eyes on her again; you must kill her and bring me her lungs and liver as tokens.'

The Huntsman obeyed, and took Snowdrop out into the forest, but when he drew his hunting-knife and was preparing to plunge it into her innocent heart, she began to cry:

'Alas! Dear Huntsman, spare my life, and I will run away into the wild forest and never come back again.'

And because of her beauty the Huntsman had pity on her and said, 'Well, run away, poor child.' *Wild beasts will soon devour you,* he thought, but still he felt as though a weight were lifted from his heart because he had not been obliged to kill her. And as, just at that moment, a young fawn came leaping by, he pierced it and took the lungs and liver as tokens to the Queen. The Cook was ordered to serve them up in pickle, and the wicked Queen ate them thinking that they were Snowdrop's.

Now the poor child was alone in the great wood, with no living soul near, and she was so frightened that she knew not what to do. Then she began to run, and ran over the sharp stones and through the brambles, while the animals passed her by without harming her. She ran as far as her feet could carry her till it was nearly evening, when she saw a little house and went in to rest. Inside, everything was small, but as neat and clean as could be. A small table covered with a white cloth stood ready with seven small plates, and by every plate was a spoon, knife, fork and cup. Seven little beds were ranged against the walls, covered with snow-white coverlets. As Snowdrop was very hungry and thirsty she ate a little bread and vegetable from each plate, and drank a little wine from each cup, for she did not want to eat up the whole of one portion. Then, being very tired, she lay down in one of the beds. She tried them all but none suited her; one was too short, another too long, all except the seventh, which was just right. She remained in it, said her prayers, and fell asleep.

When it was quite dark, the masters of the house came in. They were seven Dwarfs, who worked in the mountains digging for ore. They kindled their lights, and as soon as they could see they noticed that some one had been there, for everything was not in the order in which they had left it.

The first said, 'Who has been sitting in my chair?'

The second said, 'Who has been eating off my plate?'

The third said, 'Who has been nibbling my bread?'

The fourth said, 'Who has been eating my vegetables?'

The fifth said, 'Who has been using my fork?'

The sixth said, 'Who has been cutting with my knife?'

The seventh said, 'Who has been drinking out of my cup?'

Then the first looked and saw a slight impression on his bed, and said, 'Who has been treading on my bed?'

The others came running up and said, 'And mine, and mine.'

But the seventh, when he looked into his bed, saw Snowdrop, who lay there asleep. He called the others, who came up and cried out with

astonishment as they held their lights and gazed at Snowdrop. 'Heavens! what a beautiful child,' they said, and they were so delighted that they did not wake her up but left her asleep in bed. And the seventh Dwarf slept with his comrades, an hour with each all through the night.

When morning came Snowdrop woke up, and when she saw the seven Dwarfs she was frightened.

But they were very kind and asked her name.

'I am called Snowdrop,' she answered.

'How did you get into our house?' they asked.

Then she told them how her stepmother had wished to get rid of her, how the Huntsman had spared her life, and how she had run all day till she had found the house.

Then the Dwarfs said, 'Will you look after our household, cook, make the beds, wash, sew and knit, and keep everything neat and clean? If so, you shall stay with us and want for nothing.'

'Yes,' said Snowdrop, 'with all my heart.' And she stayed with them and kept the house in order.

In the morning they went to the mountain and searched for copper and gold, and in the evening they came back and then their meal had to be ready. All day the maiden was alone, and the good Dwarfs warned her and said, 'Beware of your stepmother, who will soon learn that you are here. Don't let anyone in.'

The Queen, having, as she imagined, eaten Snowdrop's liver and lungs, and feeling certain that she was the fairest of all, stepped in front of her Glass, and asked:

> Mirror, Mirror on the wall,
> Who is fairest of us all?

the Glass answered as usual:

> Queen, thou art fairest here, I hold,
> But Snowdrop over the fells,
> Who with the seven Dwarfs dwells,
> Is fairer still a thousandfold.

She was dismayed, for she knew that the Glass told no lies, and she saw that the Hunter had deceived her and that Snowdrop still lived. Accordingly, she began to wonder afresh how she might compass her death; for as long as she was not the fairest in the land her jealous heart left her no rest. At last she thought of a plan. She dyed her face and dressed up like an old pedlar, so that she was quite unrecognisable. In this guise she crossed over the seven mountains to the home of the seven Dwarfs and called out, 'Wares for sale.'

Snowdrop peeped out of the window and said, 'Good day, mother, what have you got to sell?'

'Good wares, fine wares,' she answered, 'laces of every colour,' and she held out one which was made of bright plaited silk.

I may let the honest woman in, thought Snowdrop, and she unbolted the door and bought the pretty lace.

'Child,' said the Old Woman, 'what a sight you are, I will lace you properly for once.'

Snowdrop made no objection, and placed herself before the Old Woman to let her lace her with the new lace. But the Old Woman laced so quickly and tightly that she took away Snowdrop's breath and she fell down as though dead.

'Now I am the fairest,' she said to herself, and hurried away.

Not long after, the seven Dwarfs came home, and were horror-struck when they saw their dear little Snowdrop lying on the floor without stirring, like one dead. When they saw she was laced too tight they cut the lace, whereupon she began to breathe and soon came back to life again. When the Dwarfs heard what had happened, they said that the Old Woman was no other than the wicked Queen. 'Take care not to let anyone in when we are not here,' they said.

Now the wicked Queen, as soon as she got home, went to the Glass and asked:

Mirror, Mirror on the wall,
Who is fairest of us all?

and it answered as usual:

> Queen, thou art fairest here, I hold,
> But Snowdrop over the fells,
> Who with the seven Dwarfs dwells,
> Is fairer still a thousandfold.

When she heard it all her blood flew to her heart, so enraged was she, for she knew that Snowdrop had come back to life again. Then she thought to herself, *I must plan something which will put an end to her.*

By means of witchcraft, in which she was skilled, she made a poisoned comb. Next she disguised herself and took the form of a different Old Woman. She crossed the mountains and came to the home of the seven Dwarfs, and knocked at the door calling out, 'Good wares to sell.'

Snowdrop looked out of the window and said, 'Go away, I must not let anyone in.'

'At least you may look,' answered the Old Woman, and she took the poisoned comb and held it up.

The child was so pleased with it that she let herself be beguiled, and opened the door.

When she had made a bargain the Old Woman said, 'Now I will comb your hair properly for once.'

Poor Snowdrop, suspecting no evil, let the Old Woman have her way, but scarcely was the poisoned comb fixed in her hair than the poison took effect, and the maiden fell down unconscious.

'You paragon of beauty,' said the wicked woman, 'now it is all over with you.' And she went away.

Happily it was near the time when the seven Dwarfs came home. When they saw Snowdrop lying on the ground as though dead, they immediately suspected her stepmother, and searched till they found the poisoned comb. No sooner had they removed it than Snowdrop came to herself again and related what had happened. They warned her again to be on her guard, and to open the door to no one.

When she got home the Queen stood before her Glass and said:

> Mirror, Mirror on the wall,
> Who is fairest of us all?

And it answered as usual:

> Queen, thou art fairest here, I hold,
> But Snowdrop over the fells,
> Who with the seven Dwarfs dwells,
> Is fairer still a thousandfold.

When she heard the Glass speak these words she trembled and quivered with rage. 'Snowdrop shall die,' she said, 'even if it cost me my own life.' Thereupon she went into a secret room, which no one ever entered but herself, and made a poisonous apple. Outwardly it was beautiful to look upon, with rosy cheeks, and every one who saw it longed for it, but whoever ate of it was certain to die. When the apple was ready she dyed her face and dressed herself like an old peasant woman and so crossed the seven hills to the Dwarfs' home. There she knocked.

Snowdrop put her head out of the window and said, 'I must not let anyone in, the seven Dwarfs have forbidden me.'

'It is all the same to me,' said the Peasant Woman. 'I shall soon get rid of my apples. There, I will give you one.'

'No; I must not take anything.'

'Are you afraid of poison?' said the woman. 'See, I will cut the apple in half: you eat the red side and I will keep the other.'

Now the apple was so cunningly painted that the red half alone was poisoned. Snowdrop longed for the apple, and when she saw the Peasant Woman eating she could hold out no longer, stretched out her hand and took the poisoned half. Scarcely had she put a bit into her mouth than she fell dead to the ground.

The Queen looked with a fiendish glance, and laughed aloud and said, 'White as snow, red as blood and black as ebony, this time the Dwarfs cannot wake you up again.' And when she got home and asked the Looking Glass:

> Mirror, Mirror on the wall,
> Who is fairest of us all?

it answered at last:

> Queen, thou'rt fairest of them all.

Then her jealous heart was at rest, as much at rest as a jealous heart can be. The Dwarfs, when they came at evening, found Snowdrop lying on the ground and not a breath escaped her lips, and she was quite dead. They lifted her up and looked to see whether any poison was to be found, unlaced her dress, combed her hair, washed her with wine and water, but it was no use; their dear child was dead.

They laid her on a bier, and all seven sat down and bewailed her and lamented over her for three whole days. Then they prepared to bury her, but she looked so fresh and living, and still had such beautiful rosy cheeks, that they said, 'We cannot bury her in the dark earth.' And so they had a transparent glass coffin made, so that she could be seen from every side, laid her inside and wrote on it in letters of gold her name and how she was a King's daughter. Then they set the coffin out on the mountain, and one of them always stayed by and watched it. And the birds came too and mourned for Snowdrop first an owl, then a raven and lastly a dove.

Now Snowdrop lay a long, long time in her coffin, looking as though she were asleep. It happened that a Prince was wandering in the wood, and came to the home of the seven Dwarfs to pass the night. He saw the coffin on the mountain and lovely Snowdrop inside, and read what was written in golden letters. Then he said to the Dwarfs, 'Let me have

the coffin; I will give you whatever you like for it.'

But they said, 'We will not give it up for all the gold of the world.'

Then he said, 'Then give it to me as a gift, for I cannot live without Snowdrop to gaze upon; and I will honour and revere it as my dearest treasure.'

When he had said these words the good Dwarfs pitied him and gave him the coffin.

The Prince bade his servants carry it on their shoulders. Now it happened that they stumbled over some brushwood, and the shock dislodged the piece of apple from Snowdrop's throat. In a short time she opened her eyes, lifted the lid of the coffin, sat up and came back to life again completely.

'O Heaven! Where am I?' she asked.

The Prince, full of joy, said, 'You are with me,' and he related what had happened, and then said, 'I love you better than all the world; come with me to my father's castle and be my wife.'

Snowdrop agreed and went with him, and their wedding was celebrated with great magnificence. Snowdrop's wicked stepmother was invited to the feast; and when she had put on her fine clothes she stepped to her Glass and asked:

Mirror, Mirror on the wall,
Who is fairest of us all?

The Glass answered:

> Queen, thou art fairest here, I hold,
> The Young Queen fairer a thousandfold.

Then the wicked woman uttered a curse, and was so terribly frightened that she didn't know what to do. Yet she had no rest: she felt obliged to go and see the Young Queen. And when she came in she recognised Snowdrop, and stood stock still with fear and terror. But iron slippers were heated over the fire, and were soon brought in with tongs and put before her. And she had to step into the red-hot shoes and dance till she fell down dead.

II

The White Snake

A LONG time ago there lived a king whose wisdom was celebrated far and wide. Nothing was unknown to him, and news of the most secret transactions seemed to reach him through the air.

Now he had one very odd habit. Every day at dinner, when the courtiers had withdrawn, and he was quite alone, a trusted Servant had to bring in another dish. It was always covered, and even the Servant did not know what it contained, nor anyone else, for the King never uncovered it till he was alone. This had gone on for a long time, when one day the Servant who carried the dish was overcome by his curiosity, and took the dish to his own room.

When he had carefully locked the door, he took the dish cover off, and saw a white snake lying on the dish.

At the sight of it, he could not resist tasting it; so he cut a piece off, and put it into his mouth.

Hardly had he tasted it, however, when he heard a wonderful whispering of delicate voices.

He went to the window and listened, and he noticed that the whispers came from the sparrows outside. They were chattering away, and telling each other all kinds of things that they had heard in the woods and fields. Eating the Snake had given him the power of understanding the language of birds and animals.

Now it happened on this day that the Queen lost her most precious ring, and suspicion fell upon this trusted Servant who went about everywhere.

The King sent for him, and threatened that if it was not found by the next day, he would be sent to prison.

In vain he protested his innocence; he was not believed.

In his grief and anxiety he went down into the courtyard and wondered how he should get out of his difficulty.

A number of ducks were lying peaceably together by a stream, stroking down their feathers with their bills, while they chattered gaily.

The Servant stood still to listen to them. They were telling each other of their morning's walks and experiences.

Then one of them said somewhat fretfully: 'I have something lying heavy on my stomach. In my haste I swallowed the Queen's ring this morning.'

The Servant quickly seized it by the neck, carried it off into the kitchen, and said to the Cook: 'Here's a fine fat duck. You had better kill it at once.'

'Yes, indeed,' said the Cook, weighing it in her hand. 'It has spared no pains in stuffing itself; it should have been roasted long ago.'

So she killed it, and cut it open, and there, sure enough, was the Queen's ring.

The Servant had now no difficulty in proving his innocence, and the King, to make up for his injustice, gave the Servant leave to ask any favour he liked, and promised him the highest post about the Court which he might desire.

The Servant, however, declined everything but a horse and some money to travel with, as he wanted to wander about for a while, to see the world.

His request being granted, he set off on his travels, and one day came to a pond, where he saw three fishes caught among the reeds and gasping for breath. Although it is said that fishes are dumb, he understood their complaint at perishing thus miserably. As he had a compassionate heart, he got off his horse and put the three captives back into the water. They wriggled in their joy, stretched up their heads above the water, and cried: 'We will remember that you saved us, and reward you for it.'

He rode on again, and after a time he seemed to hear a voice in the sand at his feet. He listened, and heard an ant king complain: 'I wish these human beings and their animals would keep out of our way. A clumsy horse has just put his hoof down upon a number of my people in the most heartless way.'

He turned his horse into a side path, and the Ant King cried: 'We will remember and reward you.'

The road now ran through a forest, and he saw a pair of ravens standing by their nest throwing out their young.

'Away with you, you gallows birds,' they were saying. 'We can't feed you any longer. You are old enough to look after yourselves.'

The poor little nestlings lay on the ground, fluttering and flapping their wings, and crying: 'We poor, helpless children, to feed ourselves, and we can't even fly! We shall die of hunger, there is nothing else for it.'

The good Youth dismounted, killed his horse with his sword, and left the carcass as food for the young ravens. They hopped along to it, and cried: 'We will remember and reward you.'

Now he had to depend upon his own legs, and after going a long way he came to a large town.

There was much noise and bustle in the streets, where a man on horseback was making a proclamation.

'The King's daughter seeks a husband, but anyone who wishes to sue for her hand must accomplish a hard task; and if he does not bring it to a successful issue, he will forfeit his life.'

Many had already attempted the task, but they had risked their lives in vain.

When the Youth saw the Princess, he was so dazzled by her beauty that he forgot all danger, at once sought an audience of the King, and announced himself as a suitor.

He was immediately led out to the seashore, and a golden ring was thrown into the water before his eyes. Then the King ordered him to fetch it out from the depths of the sea, and added: 'If you come to land without it, you will be thrown back every time till you perish in the waves.'

Everyone pitied the handsome Youth, but they had to go and leave him standing solitary on the seashore.

He was pondering over what he should do, when, all at once, he saw three fishes swimming towards him. They were no others than the very ones whose lives he had saved.

The middle one carried a mussel-shell in its mouth, which it laid on the sand at the feet of the Youth. When he picked it up, and opened it, there lay the ring.

Full of joy, he took it to the King, expecting that he would give him the promised reward.

The proud Princess, however, when she heard that he was not her equal, despised him, and demanded that he should perform yet another task.

So she went into the garden herself, and strewed ten sacks of millet seeds among the grass.

'He must pick up every one of those before the sun rises tomorrow morning,' said she. 'Not a grain must be missing.'

The Youth sat miserably in the garden, wondering how it could possibly be done. But as he could not think of a plan, he remained sadly waiting for the dawn which would bring death to him.

But when the first sunbeams fell on the garden, he saw the ten sacks full to the top, and not a grain was missing. The Ant King had come in the night with thousands and thousands of his ants, and the grateful creatures had picked up the millet and filled the sacks.

The Princess came into the garden herself, and saw with amazement that the Youth had completed the task.

But still she could not control her proud heart, and she said: 'Even if he has accomplished these two tasks, he shall not become my husband till he brings me an apple from the tree of life.'

The Youth had no idea where to find the tree of life. However, he started off, meaning to walk as far as his legs would carry him; but he had no hope of finding it.

When he had travelled through three kingdoms, he was one night passing through a great forest, and he lay down under a tree to sleep.

He heard a rustling among the branches, and a golden apple fell into his hand. At the same time three ravens flew down and perched on his knee, and said: 'We are the young ravens you saved from death. When we grew big, and heard that you were looking for the golden apple, we flew across the sea to the end of the world, where the tree of life stands, and brought you the apple.'

The Youth, delighted, started on his homeward journey, and took the golden apple to the beautiful Princess, who had now no further excuse to offer.

They divided the apple of life, and ate it together, and then her heart was filled with love for him, and they lived happily to a great age.

III

The Golden Goose

THERE was once a man who had three sons. The youngest of them was called Simpleton; he was scorned and despised by the others, and kept in the background.

The eldest son was going into the forest to cut wood, and before he started, his mother gave him a nice sweet cake and a bottle of wine to take with him, so that he might not suffer from hunger or thirst. In the wood he met a little, old, grey man, who bade him good day, and said, 'Give me a bit of the cake in your pocket, and let me have a drop of your wine. I am so hungry and thirsty.'

But the clever son said: 'If I give you my cake and wine, I shan't have enough for myself. Be off with you.'

He left the Little Man standing there, and went on his way. But he had not been long at work, cutting down a tree, before he made a false stroke, and dug the axe into his own arm, and he was obliged to go home to have it bound up.

Now, this was no accident; it was brought about by the Little Grey Man.

The second son now had to go into the forest to cut wood, and, like the eldest, his mother gave him a sweet cake and a bottle of wine. In the same way the Little Grey Man met him, and asked for a piece of his cake and a drop of his wine. But the second son made the same sensible answer, 'If I give you any, I shall have the less for myself. Be off out of my way,' and he went on.

His punishment, however, was not long delayed. After a few blows at

the tree, he hit his own leg, and had to be carried home.

Then Simpleton said, 'Let me go to cut the wood, Father.'

But his father said, 'Your brothers have only come to harm by it; you had better leave it alone. You know nothing about it.' But Simpleton begged so hard to be allowed to go that at last his father said, 'Well, off you go then. You will be wiser when you have hurt yourself.'

His mother gave him a cake which was only mixed with water and baked in the ashes, and a bottle of sour beer. When he reached the forest, like the others, he met the Little Grey Man, who greeted him, and said, 'Give me a bit of your cake and a drop of your wine. I am so hungry and thirsty.'

Simpleton answered, 'I only have a cake baked in the ashes, and some sour beer; but, if you like such fare, we will sit down and eat it together.'

So they sat down; but when Simpleton pulled out his cake it was a sweet, nice cake, and his sour beer was turned into good wine. So they ate and drank, and the Little Man said, 'As you have such a good heart, and are willing to share your goods, I will give you good luck. There stands an old tree; cut it down, and you will find something at the roots.'

So saying he disappeared.

Simpleton cut down the tree, and when it fell, lo, and behold! A goose was sitting among the roots, and its feathers were of pure gold. He picked it up, and taking it with him, went to an inn, where he meant to stay the night. The landlord had three daughters, who saw the goose, and were

very curious as to what kind of bird it could be, and wanted to get one of its golden feathers.

The eldest thought, 'There will soon be some opportunity for me to pull out one of the feathers,' and when Simpleton went outside, she took hold of its wing to pluck out a feather; but her hand stuck fast, and she could not get away.

Soon after, the second sister came up, meaning also to pluck out one of the golden feathers; but she had hardly touched her sister when she found herself held fast.

Lastly, the third one came, with the same intention, but the others screamed out, 'Keep away! For goodness' sake, keep away!'

But she, not knowing why she was to keep away, thought, *Why should*

I not be there, if they are there?

So she ran up, but as soon as she touched her sisters she had to stay hanging on to them, and they all had to pass the night like this.

In the morning, Simpleton took up the Goose under his arm, without noticing the three girls hanging on behind. They had to keep running behind, dodging his legs right and left.

In the middle of the fields they met the Parson, who, when he saw the procession, cried out: 'For shame, you bold girls! Why do you run after the lad like that? Do you call that proper behaviour?'

Then he took hold of the hand of the youngest girl to pull her away; but no sooner had he touched her than he felt himself held fast, and he, too, had to run behind.

Soon after, the Sexton came up, and, seeing his master the Parson treading on the heels of the three girls, cried out in amazement, 'Hullo, Your Reverence!

Whither away so fast? Don't forget that we have a christening!' So saying, he plucked the Parson by the sleeve, and soon found that he could not get away.

As this party of five, one behind the other, tramped on, two peasants came along the road, carrying their hoes. The Parson called them, and asked them to set the Sexton and himself free. But as soon as ever they touched the Sexton they were held fast, so now there were seven people running behind Simpleton and his goose.

By and by they reached a town, where a King ruled whose only daughter was so solemn that nothing and nobody could make her laugh.

So the King had proclaimed that whoever could make her laugh should marry her.

When Simpleton heard this he took his goose, with all his following, before her, and when she saw these seven people running, one behind another, she burst into fits of laughter, and seemed as if she could never stop.

Thereupon Simpleton asked her in marriage. But the King did not like him for a son-in-law, and he made all sorts of conditions. First, he said Simpleton must bring him a man who could drink up a cellar full of wine.

Then Simpleton at once thought of the Little Grey Man who might be able to help him, and he went out to the forest to look for him. On the very spot where the tree that he had cut down had stood, he saw a man sitting with a very sad face. Simpleton asked him what was the matter, and he answered: 'I am so thirsty, and I can't quench my thirst. I hate cold water, and I have already emptied a cask of wine; but what is a drop like that on a burning stone?'

'Well, there I can help you,' said Simpleton. 'Come with me, and you shall soon have enough to drink and to spare.'

He led him to the King's cellar, and the man set to upon the great casks, and he drank and drank till his sides ached, and by the end of the day the cellar was empty.

Then again Simpleton demanded his bride. But the King was annoyed that a wretched fellow called 'Simpleton' should have his daughter, and he made new conditions. He was now to find a man who could eat up a mountain of bread.

Simpleton did not reflect long, but went straight to the forest, and there in the self-same place sat a man tightening a strap round his body, and making a very miserable face. He said: 'I have eaten up a whole ovenful of rolls, but what is the good of that when anyone is as hungry as I am. I am never satisfied. I have to tighten my belt every day if I am not to die of hunger.'

Simpleton was delighted, and said: 'Get up and come with me. You shall have enough to eat.'

And he took him to the Court, where the King had caused all the flour in the kingdom to be brought together, and a huge mountain of bread to be baked. The Man from the forest sat down before it and began to eat, and at the end of the day the whole mountain had disappeared.

Now, for the third time, Simpleton asked for his bride. But again the King tried to find an excuse, and demanded a ship which could sail on land as well as at sea.

'As soon as you sail up in it, you shall have my daughter,' he said.

Simpleton went straight to the forest, and there sat the Little Grey Man to whom he had given his cake. The Little Man said: 'I have eaten and drunk for you, and now I will give you the ship, too. I do it all because you were merciful to me.'

Then he gave him the ship which could sail on land as well as at sea, and when the King saw it he could no longer withhold his daughter. The marriage was celebrated, and, at the King's death, Simpleton inherited the kingdom, and lived long and happily with his wife.

IV

The Three Languages

There once lived in Switzerland an old count, who had an only son; but he was very stupid, and could learn nothing. So his father said to him: 'Listen to me, my son. I can get nothing into your head, try as hard as I may. You must go away from here, and I will hand you over to a renowned professor for a whole year.' At the end of the year he came home again, and his father asked: 'Now, my son, what have you learnt?'

'Father, I have learnt the language of dogs.'

'Mercy on us!' cried his father, 'is that all you have learnt? I will send you away again to another professor in a different town.' The youth was taken there, and remained with this professor also for another year. When he came back his father asked him again: 'My son, what have you learnt?'

He answered: 'I have learnt bird language.'

Then the father flew into a rage, and said: 'Oh, you hopeless creature, have you been spending all this precious time and learnt nothing? Aren't you ashamed to come into my presence? I will send you to a third professor, but if you learn nothing this time, I won't be your father any longer.'

The son stopped with the third professor in the same way for a whole year, and when he came home again and his father asked, 'My son, what have you learnt?' he answered: 'My dear father, this year I have learnt frog language.'

Thereupon his father flew into a fearful passion, and said: 'This creature is my son no longer. I turn him out of the house and command you to lead him into the forest and take his life.'

They led him forth, but when they were about to kill him, for pity's sake they could not do it, and let him go. Then they cut out the eyes and tongue of a fawn, in order that they might take back proof to the old Count.

The Youth wandered about, and at length came to a castle, where he begged a night's lodging.

'Very well,' said the Lord of the castle. 'If you like to pass the night down there in the old tower, you may; but I warn you that it will be at the risk of your life, for it is full of savage dogs. They bark and howl without ceasing, and at certain hours they must have a man thrown to them, and they devour him at once.'

The whole neighbourhood was distressed by the scourge, but no one could do anything to remedy it. But the youth was not a bit afraid and said: 'Just let me go down to these barking dogs, and give me something that I can throw to them; they won't do me any harm.'

As he would not have anything else, they gave him some food for the savage dogs, and took him down to the tower.

The dogs did not bark at him when he entered, but ran round him wagging their tails in a most friendly manner, ate the food he gave them, and did not so much as touch a hair of his head.

The next morning, to the surprise of everyone, he made his appearance again, and said to the Lord of the castle, 'The dogs have revealed to me in their own language why they live there and bring mischief to the country. They are enchanted, and obliged to guard a great treasure which is hidden under the tower, and will get no rest till it has been dug up; and how that has to be done I have also learnt from them.'

Everyone who heard this was delighted, and the Lord of the castle said he would adopt him as a son if he accomplished the task successfully. He went down to the tower again, and as he knew how to set to work he accomplished his task, and brought out a chest full of gold. The howling of the savage dogs was from that time forward heard no more. They entirely disappeared, and the country was delivered from the scourge.

After a time, he took it into his head to go to Rome. On the way he passed a swamp, in which a number of frogs were croaking. He listened, and when he heard what they were saying he became quite pensive and sad.

At last he reached Rome, at a moment when the Pope had just died, and there was great doubt among the Cardinals whom they ought to name as his successor. They agreed at last that the man to whom some divine miracle should be manifested ought to be chosen as Pope. Just as they had come to this decision, the young Count entered the church, and suddenly two snow-white doves flew down and alighted on his shoulders.

The clergy recognised in this the sign from Heaven, and asked him on the spot whether he would be Pope.

He was undecided, and knew not whether he was worthy of the post; but the doves told him that he might accept, and at last he said, 'Yes.'

Thereupon he was anointed and consecrated, and so was fulfilled what he had heard from the frogs on the way, which had disturbed him so much – namely, that he should become Pope.

Then he had to chant mass, and did not know one word of it. But the two doves sat upon his shoulders and whispered it to him.

V

THE GOOSE-GIRL

THERE was once an old queen whose husband had been dead for many years, and she had a very beautiful daughter. When she grew up she was betrothed to a prince in a distant country. When the time came for the maiden to be sent into this distant country to be married, the old Queen packed up quantities of clothes and jewels, gold and silver, cups and ornaments, and, in fact, everything suitable to a royal outfit, for she loved her daughter very dearly.

She also sent a waiting-woman to travel with her, and to put her hand into that of the bridegroom. They each had a horse. The Princess's horse was called Falada, and it could speak.

When the hour of departure came, the old Queen went to her bedroom and with a sharp little knife cut her finger and made it bleed. Then she held a piece of white cambric under it, and let three drops of blood fall on to it. This cambric she gave to her daughter, and said, 'Dear child, take good care of this; it will stand you in good stead on the journey.' They then bade each other a sorrowful farewell. The Princess hid the cambric in her bosom, mounted her horse, and set out to her bridegroom's country.

When they had ridden for a time the Princess became very thirsty, and said to the Waiting-woman, 'Get down and fetch me some water in my cup from the stream. I must have something to drink.'

'If you are thirsty,' said the Waiting-woman, 'dismount yourself, lie down by the water and drink. I don't choose to be your servant.'

So, in her great thirst, the Princess dismounted and stooped down to the stream and drank, as she might not have her golden cup. The poor Princess said, 'Alas!' and the drops of blood answered, 'If your mother knew this, it would break her heart.'

The royal bride was humble, so she said nothing, but mounted her horse again. Then they rode several miles further; but the day was warm, the sun was scorching, and the Princess was soon thirsty again.

When they reached a river she called out again to her Waiting-woman, 'Get down, and give me some water in my golden cup!'

She had forgotten all about the rude words which had been said to her. But the Waiting-woman answered more haughtily than ever, 'If you want to drink, get the water for yourself. I won't be your servant.'

Being very thirsty, the Princess dismounted, and knelt by the flowing water. She cried, and said, 'Ah, me!' and the drops of blood answered, 'If your mother knew this it would break her heart.'

While she stooped over the water to drink, the piece of cambric with the drops of blood on it fell out of her bosom, and floated away on the stream; but she never noticed this in her great fear. The Waiting-woman, however, had seen it, and rejoiced at getting more power over the bride, who, by losing the drops of blood, had become weak and powerless.

Now, when she was about to mount her horse Falada again, the Waiting-woman said, 'By rights, Falada belongs to me; this nag will do for you!'

The poor little Princess was obliged to give way. Then the Waiting-woman, in a harsh voice, ordered her to take off her royal robes, and to put on her own mean garments. Finally, she forced her to swear before heaven that she would not tell a creature at the Court what had taken place. Had she not taken the oath she would have been killed on the spot. But Falada saw all this and marked it.

The Waiting-woman then mounted Falada and put the real bride on her poor nag, and they continued their journey.

There was great rejoicing when they arrived at the castle. The Prince hurried towards them, and lifted the Waiting-woman from her horse, thinking she was his bride. She was led upstairs, but the real Princess had to stay below.

The old King looked out of the window and saw the delicate, pretty little creature standing in the courtyard; so he went to the bridal apartments and asked the bride about her companion, who was left standing in the courtyard, and wished to know who she was.

Arthur Rackham · 1909

'I picked her up on the way, and brought her with me for company. Give the girl something to do to keep her from idling.'

But the old King had no work for her, and could not think of anything. At last he said, 'I have a little lad who looks after the geese; she may help him.'

The boy was called little Conrad, and the real bride was sent with him to look after the geese.

Soon after, the false bride said to the Prince, 'Dear husband, I pray you do me a favour.'

He answered, 'That will I gladly.'

'Well, then, let the knacker be called to cut off the head of the horse I rode; it angered me on the way.'

Really, she was afraid that the horse would speak, and tell of her treatment of the Princess. So it was settled, and the faithful Falada had to die.

When this came to the ear of the real Princess, she promised the knacker a piece of gold if he would do her a slight service. There was a great dark gateway to the town, through which she had to pass every morning and evening. 'Would he nail up Falada's head in this gateway, so that she might see him as she passed?'

The knacker promised to do as she wished, and when the horse's head was cut off, he hung it up in the dark gateway. In the early morning, when she and Conrad went through the gateway, she said in passing:

Alas! Dear Falada, there thou hangest.

And the Head answered:

> Alas! Queen's daughter, there thou gangest.
> If thy mother knew thy fate,
> Her heart would break with grief so great.

Then they passed on out of the town, right into the fields, with the geese. When they reached the meadow, the Princess sat down on the grass and let down her hair. It shone like pure gold, and when little Conrad saw it, he was so delighted that he wanted to pluck some out; but she said:

> Blow, blow, little breeze,
> And Conrad's hat seize.
> Let him join in the chase
> While away it is whirled,
> Till my tresses are curled
> And I rest in my place.

Then a strong wind sprang up, which blew away Conrad's hat right over the fields, and he had to run after it. When he came back, she had finished combing her hair, and it was all put up again; so he could not get a single hair. This made him very sulky, and he would not say another word to her. And they tended the geese till evening, when they went home.

Next morning, when they passed under the gateway, the Princess said:

Alas! Dear Falada, there thou hangest.

Falada answered:

Alas! Queen's daughter, there thou gangest.
If thy mother knew thy fate,
Her heart would break with grief so great.

Again, when they reached the meadows, the Princess undid her hair and began combing it. Conrad ran to pluck some out; but she said quickly:

Blow, blow, little breeze,
And Conrad's hat seize.
Let him join in the chase
While away it is whirled,
Till my tresses are curled
And I rest in my place.

The wind sprang up and blew Conrad's hat far away over the fields, and he had to run after it. When he came back the hair was all put up again, and he could not pull a single hair out. And they tended the geese till the evening. When they got home Conrad went to the old King, and said, 'I won't tend the geese with that maiden again.'

'Why not?' asked the King.

'Oh, she vexes me every day.'

The old King then ordered him to say what she did to vex him.

Conrad said, 'In the morning, when we pass under the dark gateway with the geese, she talks to a horse's head which is hung up on the wall. She says:

Alas! Falada, there thou hangest,

and the Head answers:

Alas! Queen's daughter, there thou gangest.
If thy mother knew thy fate,
Her heart would break with grief so great.

Then Conrad went on to tell the King all that happened in the meadow, and how he had to run after his hat in the wind.

The old King ordered Conrad to go out next day as usual. Then he placed himself behind the dark gateway, and heard the Princess speaking to Falada's head. He also followed her into the field, and hid himself behind a bush, and with his own eyes he saw the Goose-girl and the lad come driving the geese into the field. Then, after a time, he saw the girl let down her hair, which glittered in the sun. Directly after this, she said:

Blow, blow, little breeze,
And Conrad's hat seize.
Let him join in the chase
While away it is whirled,
Till my tresses are curled
And I rest in my place.

Then came a puff of wind, which carried off Conrad's hat and he had to run after it. While he was away, the maiden combed and did up her hair; and all this the old King observed. Thereupon he went away unnoticed; and in the evening, when the Goose-girl came home, he called her aside and asked why she did all these things.

'That I may not tell you, nor may I tell any human creature; for I have sworn it under the open sky, because if I had not done so I should have lost my life.'

He pressed her sorely, and gave her no peace, but he could get nothing out of her. Then he said, 'If you won't tell me, then tell your sorrows to the iron stove there.' And he went away.

She crept up to the stove, and, beginning to weep and lament, unburdened her heart to it, and said: 'Here I am, forsaken by all the world, and yet I am a Princess. A false waiting-woman brought me to such a pass that I had to take off my royal robes. Then she took my place with my bridegroom, while I have to do mean service as a goose-girl. If my mother knew it she would break her heart.'

The old King stood outside by the pipes of the stove, and heard all that she said. Then he came back, and told her to go away from the stove. He caused royal robes to be put upon her, and her beauty was a marvel. The old King called his son, and told him that he had a false bride – she was only a waiting-woman; but the true bride was here, the so-called Goose-girl.

The young Prince was charmed with her youth and beauty. A great banquet was prepared, to which all the courtiers and good friends were bidden. The bridegroom sat at the head of the table, with the Princess on one side and the Waiting-Woman at the other; but she was dazzled, and did not recognise the Princess in her brilliant apparel.

When they had eaten and drunk and were all very merry, the old King put a riddle to the Waiting-woman. 'What does a person deserve who deceives their master?' telling the whole story, and ending by asking, 'What doom do they deserve?'

The false bride answered, 'No better than this. They must be put stark naked into a barrel stuck with nails, and be dragged along by two white horses from street to street till dead.'

'That is your own doom,' said the King, 'and the judgement shall be carried out.'

When the sentence was fulfilled, the young Prince married his true bride, and they ruled their kingdom together in peace and happiness.

VI

Rumpelstiltskin

THERE was once a miller who was very poor, but he had a beautiful daughter. Now, it fell out that he had occasion to speak with the King, and, in order to give himself an air of importance, he said: 'I have a daughter who can spin gold out of straw.'

The King said to the Miller: 'That is an art in which I am much interested. If your daughter is as skilful as you say she is, bring her to my castle tomorrow, and I will put her to the test.'

Accordingly, when the girl was brought to the castle, the King conducted her to a chamber which was quite full of straw, gave her a spinning wheel and winder, and said, 'Now, set to work, and if between tonight and tomorrow at dawn you have not spun this straw into gold you must die.' Thereupon he carefully locked the door of the chamber, and she remained alone.

There sat the unfortunate Miller's daughter, and for the life of her did not know what to do. She had not the least idea how to spin straw into gold, and she became more and more distressed, until at last she began to weep. Then all at once the door sprang open, and in stepped a little mannikin, who said: 'Good evening, Mistress Miller, what are you weeping so for?'

'Alas!' answered the Maiden, 'I've got to spin gold out of straw, and don't know how to do it.'

Then the Mannikin said, 'What will you give me if I spin it for you?'

'My necklace,' said the Maid.

The little Man took the necklace, sat down before the spinning wheel, and whir – whir – whir, in a trice the reel was full.

Then he fixed another reel, and whir – whir – whir, thrice round, and that too was full; and so it went on until morning, when all the straw was spun and all the reels were full of gold.

Immediately at sunrise, the King came, and when he saw the gold he was astonished and much pleased, but his mind became only the more avaricious. So he had the Miller's daughter taken to another chamber, larger than the former one, and full of straw, and he ordered her to spin it also in one night, as she valued her life.

The Maiden was at her wit's end and began to weep. Then again the door sprang open, and the little Mannikin appeared, and said, 'What will you give me if I spin the straw into gold for you?'

'The ring off my finger,' answered the Maiden.

The little man took the ring, began to whir again at the wheel, and had by morning spun all the straw into gold.

The King was delighted at sight of the masses of gold, but was not even yet satisfied. So he had the Miller's daughter taken to a still larger chamber, full of straw, and said, 'This must you tonight spin into gold, but if you succeed you shall become my queen.' *Even if she is only a Miller's daughter,* thought he, *I shan't find a richer woman in the whole world.*

When the girl was alone the little Man came again, and said for the third time, 'What will you give me if I spin the straw for you this time?'

'I have nothing more that I can give,' answered the girl.

'Well, promise me your first child if you become queen.'

Who knows what may happen, thought the Miller's daughter; but she did not see any other way of getting out of the difficulty, so she promised the little Man what he demanded, and in return he spun the straw into gold once more.

When the King came in the morning, and found everything as he had wished, he celebrated his marriage with her, and the Miller's daughter became queen.

About a year afterwards a beautiful child was born, but the Queen had forgotten all about the little Man. However, he suddenly entered her chamber, and said, 'Now, give me what you promised.'

The Queen was terrified, and offered the little Man all the wealth of the kingdom if he would let her keep the child. But the Mannikin said, 'No. I would rather have some living thing than all the treasures of the world.' Then the Queen began to moan and weep to such an extent that the little Man felt sorry for her. 'I will give you three days,' said he, 'and if within that time you discover my name you shall keep the child.'

Then during the night the Queen called to mind all the names that she had ever heard, and sent a messenger all over the country to inquire far and wide what other names there were. When the little Man came on the next day, she began with Caspar, Melchoir, Balthazar, and mentioned all the names which she knew, one after the other; but at every one the little Man said: 'No; that's not my name.'

The second day she had inquiries made all round the neighbourhood for the names of people living there, and suggested to the little Man all the most unusual and strange names.

'Perhaps your name is Cowribs, Spindleshanks or Spiderlegs?'

But he answered every time, 'No; that's not my name.'

On the third day the messenger came back and said: 'I haven't been able to find any new names, but as I came round the corner of a wood on a lofty mountain, where the fox says goodnight to the hare, I saw a little house, and in front of the house a fire was burning; and around the fire an

indescribably ridiculous little man was leaping, hopping on one leg, and singing:

> Today I bake; tomorrow I brew my beer;
> The next day I will bring the Queen's child here.
> Ah! Lucky 'tis that not a soul doth know
> That Rumpelstiltskin is my name, ho! Ho!'

Then you can imagine how delighted the Queen was when she heard the name, and when presently afterwards the little Man came in and asked, 'Now, Your Majesty, what is my name?' at first she asked:

'Is your name Tom?'

'No.'

'Is it Dick?'

'No.'

'Is it, by chance, Rumpelstiltskin?'

'The devil told you that! The devil told you that!' shrieked the little Man; and in his rage stamped his right foot into the ground so deep that he sank up to his waist.

Then, in his passion, he seized his left leg with both hands, and tore himself asunder in the middle.

VII

The Valiant Tailor

A TAILOR was sitting on his table at the window one summer morning. He was a good fellow, and stitched with all his might. A peasant woman came down the street, crying, 'Good jam for sale! Good jam for sale!'

This had a pleasant sound in the Tailor's ears; he put his pale face out of the window, and cried, 'You'll find a sale for your wares up here, good Woman.'

The Woman went up the three steps to the Tailor, with the heavy basket on her head, and he made her unpack all her pots. He examined them all, lifted them up, smelt them, and at last said, 'The jam seems good; weigh me out four ounces, good Woman, and should it come over the quarter pound, it will be all the same to me.'

The Woman, who had hoped for a better sale, gave him what he asked for, but went away cross, and grumbling to herself.

'That jam will be a blessing to me,' cried the Tailor; 'it will give me strength and power.' He brought his bread out of the cupboard, cut a whole slice, and spread the jam on it. 'It won't be a bitter morsel,' said he, 'but I will finish this waistcoat before I stick my teeth into it.'

He put the bread down by his side, and went on with his sewing, but in his joy the stitches got bigger and bigger. The smell of the jam rose to the wall, where the flies were clustered in swarms, and tempted them to come down, and they settled on the jam in masses.

'Ah! Who invited you?' cried the Tailor, chasing away his unbidden guests. But the flies, who did not understand his language, were not to be got rid of so easily, and came back in greater numbers than ever. At last the Tailor came to the end of his patience, and seizing a bit of cloth, he cried, 'Wait a bit, and I'll give it you!' So saying, he struck out at them mercilessly.

When he looked, he found no fewer than seven dead and motionless. 'So that's the kind of fellow you are,' he said, admiring his own valour. 'The whole town shall know of this.'

In great haste he cut out a belt for himself, and stitched on it, in big letters, *Seven at one blow!* 'The town!' he then said, 'the whole world shall know of it!' And his heart wagged for very joy like the tail of a lamb. The Tailor fastened the belt round his waist, and wanted to start out into the world at once; he found his workshop too small for his valour. Before starting, he searched the house to see if there was anything to take with him. He only found an old cheese, but this he put into his pocket. By the gate he saw a bird entangled in a thicket, and he put that into his pocket with the cheese. Then he boldly took to the road, and as he was light and active, he felt no fatigue. The road led up a mountain, and when he reached the highest point, he found a huge giant sitting there comfortably looking round him.

The Tailor went pluckily up to him, and addressed him.

'Good day, Comrade, you are sitting there surveying the wide world, I suppose. I am just on my way to try my luck. Do you feel inclined to go with me?'

The Giant looked scornfully at the Tailor, and said, 'You jackanapes! You miserable ragamuffin!'

'That may be,' said the Tailor, unbuttoning his coat and showing the Giant his belt. 'You may just read what kind of fellow I am.'

The Giant read, *Seven at one blow,* and thought that it was people the Tailor had slain; so it gave him a certain amount of respect for the little fellow. Still, he thought he would try him; so he picked up a stone and squeezed it till the water dropped out of it.

'Do that,' he said, 'if you have the strength.'

'No more than that!' said the Tailor. 'Why, it's a mere joke to me.'

He put his hand into his pocket, and pulling out the bit of soft cheese, he squeezed it till the moisture ran out.

'I guess that will equal you,' said he.

The Giant did not know what to say, and could not have believed it of the little man.

Then the Giant picked up a stone, and threw it up so high that one could scarcely follow it with the eye.

'Now, then, you sample of a mannikin, do that after me.'

'Well thrown!' said the Tailor, 'but the stone fell to the ground again. Now I will throw one for you which will never come back again.'

So saying, he put his hand into his pocket, took out the bird, and threw it into the air. The bird, rejoiced at its freedom, soared into the air, and was never seen again.

'What do you think of that, Comrade?' asked the Tailor.

'You can certainly throw. But now we will see if you are in a condition to carry anything,' said the Giant.

He led the Tailor to a mighty oak which had been felled, and which lay upon the ground.

'If you are strong enough, help me out of the wood with this tree,' he said.

'Willingly,' answered the little man. 'You take the trunk on your shoulder, and I will take the branches; they must certainly be the heaviest.'

The Giant accordingly took the trunk on his shoulder; but the Tailor seated himself on one of the branches, and the Giant, who could not look

7 at on

round, had to carry the whole tree, and the Tailor into the bargain. The Tailor was very merry on the end of the tree, and whistled 'Three Tailors rode merrily out of the town', as if tree-carrying were a joke to him.

When the Giant had carried the tree some distance, he could go no further, and exclaimed, 'Look out, I am going to drop the tree.'

The Tailor sprang to the ground with great agility, and seized the tree with both arms, as if he had been carrying it all the time. He said to the Giant: 'Big fellow as you are, you can't carry a tree.'

After a time they went on together, and when they came to a cherry tree, the Giant seized the top branches, where the cherries ripened first, bent them down, put them in the Tailor's hand, and told him to eat. The Tailor, however, was much too weak to hold the tree, and when the Giant let go, the tree sprang back, carrying the Tailor with it into the air. When he reached the ground again, without any injury, the Giant said, 'What's this? Haven't you the strength to hold a feeble sapling?'

'It's not strength that's wanting,' answered the Tailor. 'Do you think that would be anything to one who killed seven at a blow? I sprang over the tree because some sportsmen were shooting among the bushes. Spring after me if you like.'

The Giant made the attempt, but he could not clear the tree, and stuck among the branches. So here, too, the Tailor had the advantage of him.

The Giant said, 'If you are such a gallant fellow, come with me to our cave, and stay the night with us.'

The Tailor was quite willing, and went with him. When they reached the cave, they found several other giants sitting round a fire, and each one held a roasted sheep in his hand, which he was eating. The Tailor looked about him, and thought, *It is much more roomy here than in my workshop.*

The Giant showed him a bed, and told him to lie down and have a good sleep. The bed was much too big for the Tailor, so he did not lie down in it, but crept into a corner. At midnight, when the Giant thought the Tailor would be in a heavy sleep, he got up, took a big oak club, and with one blow crashed right through the bed, and thought he had put an end to the grasshopper. Early in the morning the giants went out into the woods, forgetting all about the Tailor, when all at once he appeared before them, as lively as possible. They were terrified, and thinking he would strike them all dead, they ran off as fast as ever they could.

The Tailor went on his way, always following his own pointed nose. When he had walked for a long time, he came to the courtyard of a royal palace. He was so tired that he lay down on the grass and went to sleep. While he lay and slept, the people came and inspected him on all sides, and they read on his belt, *Seven at one blow.* 'Alas!' they said, 'why does this great warrior come here in time of peace; he must be a mighty man.'

They went to the King and told him about it; and they were of opinion that, should war break out, he would be a useful and powerful man, who should on no account be allowed to depart. This advice pleased the King, and he sent one of his courtiers to the Tailor to offer him a military appointment when he woke up. The messenger remained standing by the

Tailor, till he opened his eyes and stretched himself, and then he made the offer.

'For that very purpose have I come,' said the Tailor. 'I am quite ready to enter the King's service.'

So he was received with honour, and a special dwelling was assigned to him.

The soldiers, however, bore him a grudge, and wished him a thousand miles away. 'What will be the end of it?' they said to each other. 'When we quarrel with him, and he strikes out, seven of us will fall at once. One of us can't cope with him.' So they took a resolve, and went all together to the King, and asked for their discharge. 'We are not made,' said they, 'to hold our own with a man who strikes seven at one blow.'

It grieved the King to lose all his faithful servants for the sake of one man; he wished he had never set eyes on the Tailor, and was quite ready to let him go. He did not dare, however, to give him his dismissal, for he was afraid that he would kill him and all his people, and place himself on the throne. He pondered over it for a long time, and at last he thought of a plan. He sent for the Tailor, and said that as he was so great a warrior, he would make him an offer. In a forest in his kingdom lived two giants, who, by robbery, murder, burning and laying waste, did much harm. No one dared approach them without being in danger of his life. If he could subdue and kill these two giants, he would give him his only daughter to be his wife, and half his kingdom as a dowry; also he would give him a hundred horsemen to accompany and help him.

That would be something for a man like me, thought the Tailor. *A beautiful Princess and half a kingdom are not offered to one every day.* 'Oh yes,' was his answer, 'I will soon subdue the giants, and that without the hundred horsemen. He who slays seven at a blow need not fear two.' The Tailor set out at once, accompanied by the hundred horsemen; but when he came to the edge of the forest, he said to his followers, 'Wait here, I will soon make an end of the giants by myself.'

Then he disappeared into the wood; he looked about to the right and to the left. Before long he espied both the giants lying under a tree, fast asleep and snoring. Their snores were so tremendous that they made the branches of the tree dance up and down. The Tailor, who was no fool, filled his pockets with stones, and climbed up the tree. When he got half-way up, he slipped on to a branch just above the sleepers, and then hurled the stones, one after another, on to one of them.

It was some time before the Giant noticed anything; then he woke up, pushed his companion, and said, 'What are you hitting me for?'

'You're dreaming,' said the other. 'I didn't hit you.' They went to sleep again, and the Tailor threw a stone at the other one. 'What's that?' he cried. 'What are you throwing at me?'

'I'm not throwing anything,' answered the first one, with a growl.

They quarrelled over it for a time, but as they were sleepy, they made it up, and their eyes closed again.

The Tailor began his game again, picked out his biggest stone, and threw it at the first giant as hard as he could.

'This is too bad,' said the Giant, flying up like a madman. He pushed his companion against the tree with such violence that it shook. The other paid him back in the same coin, and they worked themselves up into such a rage that they tore up trees by the roots, and hacked at each other till they both fell dead upon the ground.

Then the Tailor jumped down from his perch. 'It was very lucky,' he said, 'that they did not tear up the tree I was sitting on, or I should have had to spring on to another like a squirrel. But we are nimble fellows.' He drew his sword, and gave each of the giants two or three cuts in the chest. Then he went out to the horsemen, and said, 'The work is done. I have given both of them the finishing stroke, but it was a difficult job. In their distress they tore trees up by the root to defend themselves; but all that's no good when a man like me comes, who slays seven at a blow.'

'Are you not wounded?' then asked the horsemen.

'There was no danger,' answered the Tailor. 'Not a hair of my head was touched.'

The Horsemen would not believe him, and rode into the forest to see. There, right enough, lay the giants in pools of blood, and, round about them, the uprooted trees.

The Tailor now demanded his promised reward from the King; but he, in the meantime, had repented of this promise, and was again trying to think of a plan to shake him off.

'Before I give you my daughter and the half of my kingdom, you must perform one more doughty deed. There is a unicorn, which runs about in the forests doing vast damage; you must capture it.'

'I have even less fear of one unicorn than of two giants. Seven at one stroke is my style.' He took a rope and an axe, and went into the wood, and told his followers to stay outside. He did not have long to wait. The Unicorn soon appeared, and dashed towards the Tailor, as if it meant to run him through with its horn on the spot. 'Softly, softly,' cried the Tailor. 'Not so fast.' He stood still, and waited till the animal got quite near, and then he very nimbly dodged behind a tree. The unicorn rushed at the tree, and ran its horn so hard into the trunk that it had not strength to pull it out again, and so it was caught. 'Now I have the prey,' said the Tailor, coming from behind the tree. He fastened the rope round the creature's neck, and, with his axe, released the horn from the tree. When this was done he led the animal away, and took it to the King.

Still the King would not give him the promised reward, but made a third demand of him. Before the marriage, the Tailor must catch a boar, which did much damage in the woods: the huntsmen were to help him.

'Willingly,' said the Tailor. 'That will be mere child's play.'

He did not take the huntsmen into the wood with him, at which they were well pleased, for they had already more than once had such a reception from the boar that they had no wish to encounter him again. When the boar saw the Tailor, it flew at him with foaming mouth, and, gnashing its teeth, tried to throw him to the ground; but the nimble hero darted into a little chapel which stood near. He jumped out again immediately by the window. The boar rushed in after the Tailor; but he by this time was hopping about outside, and quickly shut the door upon the boar. So the raging animal was caught, for it was far too heavy and clumsy to jump out of the window. The Tailor called the huntsmen up to see the captive with their own eyes.

The hero then went to the King, who was now obliged to keep his word, whether he liked it or not; so he handed over his daughter and half his kingdom to him. Had he known that it was no warrior but only a Tailor who stood before him, he would have taken it even more to heart. The marriage was held with much pomp, but little joy, and a King was made out of a Tailor.

After a time the young Queen heard her husband talking in his sleep, and saying, 'Apprentice, bring me the waistcoat and patch the trousers, or I will break the yard measure over your head.' So in this manner she discovered the young gentleman's origin. In the morning she complained to the King, and begged him to rid her of a husband who was nothing more than a Tailor.

The King comforted her, and said, 'Tonight, leave your bedroom door open. My servants shall stand outside, and when he is asleep they shall go in and bind him. They shall then carry him away, and put him on board a ship which will take him far away.'

The lady was satisfied with this; but the Tailor's armourbearer, who was attached to his young lord, told him the whole plot.

'I will put a stop to their plan,' said the Tailor.

At night he went to bed as usual with his wife. When she thought he was asleep, she got up, opened the door, and went to bed again. The Tailor, who had only pretended to be asleep, began to cry out in a clear voice, 'Apprentice, bring me the waistcoat and you patch the trousers, or I will break the yard measure over your head. I have slain seven at a blow, killed two giants, led captive a unicorn, and caught a boar; should I be afraid of those who are standing outside my chamber door?'

When they heard the Tailor speaking like this, the servants were overcome by fear, and ran away as if wild animals were after them, and none of them would venture near him again.

So the Tailor remained a King till the day of his death.

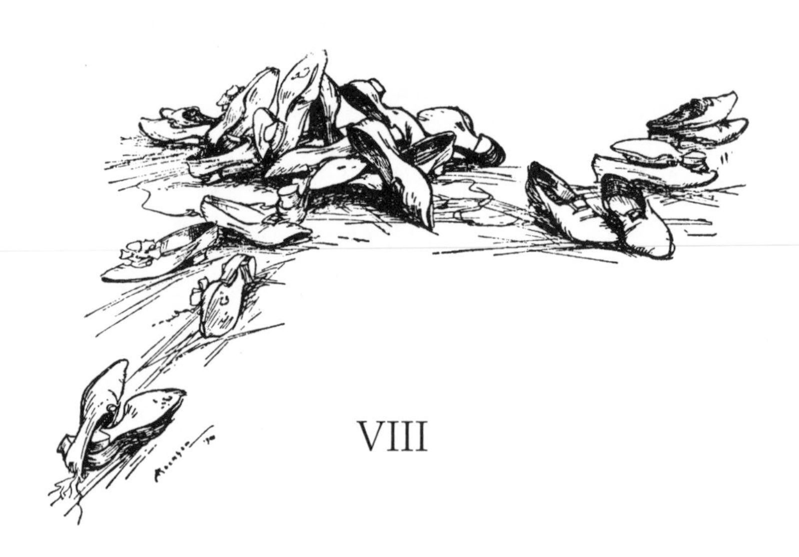

VIII

THE TWELVE DANCING PRINCESSES

THERE was once a king who had twelve daughters, each more beautiful than the other. They slept together in a hall where their beds stood close to one another; and at night, when they had gone to bed, the King locked the door and bolted it. But when he unlocked it in the morning, he noticed that their shoes had been danced to pieces, and nobody could explain how it happened. So the King sent out a proclamation saying that any one who could discover where the princesses did their night's dancing should choose one of them to be his wife and should reign after his death; but whoever presented himself, and failed to make the discovery after three days and nights, was to forfeit his life.

A prince soon presented himself and offered to take the risk. He was well received, and at night was taken into a room adjoining the hall where the princesses slept. His bed was made up there, and he was to watch and see where they went to dance; so that they could not do anything, or go anywhere else, the door of his room was left open, too. But the eyes of the Prince grew heavy, and he fell asleep. When he woke up in the morning all the twelve had been dancing, for the soles of their shoes were full of holes. The second and third evenings passed with the same results, and then the Prince found no mercy, and his head was cut off. Many others came after him and offered to take the risk, but they all had to lose their lives.

Now it happened that a poor soldier, who had been wounded and could no longer serve, found himself on the road to the town where the King lived. There he fell in with an old woman who asked him where he intended to go.

'I really don't know, myself,' he said; and added, in fun, 'I should like to discover where the King's daughters dance their shoes into holes, and after that to become King.'

'That is not so difficult,' said the old woman. 'You must not drink the wine, which will be brought to you in the evening, but must pretend to be fast asleep.' Whereupon she gave him a short cloak, saying: 'When you wear this you will be invisible, and then you can slip out after the twelve princesses.'

As soon as the Soldier heard this good advice he took it up seriously, plucked up courage, appeared before the King, and offered himself as suitor. He was as well received as the others, and was dressed in royal garments.

In the evening, when bedtime came, he was conducted to the ante-room. As he was about to go to bed the eldest Princess appeared, bringing him a cup of wine; but he had fastened a sponge under his chin and let the wine run down into it, so that he did not drink one drop. Then he lay down, and when he had been quiet a little while he began to snore as though in the deepest sleep.

The twelve princesses heard him, and laughed. The eldest said: 'He, too, must forfeit his life.'

Then they got up, opened cupboards, chests and cases and brought out their beautiful dresses. They decked themselves before the glass, skipping about and revelling in the prospect of the dance. Only the youngest sister said: 'I don't know what it is. You may rejoice, but I feel so strange; a misfortune is certainly hanging over us.'

'You are a little goose,' answered the eldest; 'you are always frightened. Have you forgotten how many princes have come here in vain? Why, I need not have given the Soldier a sleeping draught at all; the blockhead would never have awakened.'

When they were all ready they looked at the Soldier; but his eyes were shut and he did not stir. So they thought they would soon be quite safe. Then the eldest went up to one of the beds and knocked on it; it sank into the earth, and they descended through the opening, one after another, the eldest first.

The Soldier, who had noticed everything, did not hesitate long, but threw on his cloak and went down behind the youngest. Halfway down he trod on her dress. She was frightened, and said: 'What was that? Who is holding on to my dress?'

'Don't be so foolish. You must have caught on a nail,' said the eldest. Then they went right down, and when they got quite underground, they stood in a marvellously beautiful avenue of trees; all the leaves were silver, and glittered and shone.

The Soldier thought, *I must take away some token with me*. And as he broke off a twig, a sharp crack came from the tree.

The youngest cried out, 'All is not well; did you hear that sound?'

'Those are triumphal salutes, because we shall soon have released our princes,' said the eldest.

Next they came to an avenue where all the leaves were of gold, and, at last, into a third, where they were of shining diamonds. From both these he broke off a twig, and there was a crack each time which made the youngest Princess start with terror; but the eldest maintained that the sounds were only triumphal salutes. They went on faster, and came to a great lake. Close to the bank lay twelve little boats, and in every boat sat a handsome prince. They had expected the Twelve Princesses, and each took one with him; and the Soldier seated himself by the youngest.

Then said the Prince, 'I don't know why, but the boat is much heavier today, and I am obliged to row with all my strength to get it along.'

'I wonder why it is,' said the youngest, 'unless, perhaps, it is the hot weather; it is strangely hot.'

On the opposite side of the lake stood a splendid brightly lighted castle, from which came the sound of the joyous music of trumpets and drums. They rowed across, and every prince danced with his love; and the Soldier danced too, unseen. If one of the princesses held a cup of wine he drank out of it, so that it was empty when she lifted it to her lips. This frightened the youngest one, but the eldest always silenced her. They danced till three next morning, when their shoes were danced into holes, and they were obliged to stop. The princes took them back across the lake, and this time the Soldier took his seat beside the eldest. On the bank they said farewell to their princes, and promised to come again the next night. When they got to the steps, the Soldier ran on ahead, lay down in bed, and when the twelve came lagging by, slowly and wearily, he began to snore again, very loud, so that they said, 'We are quite safe as far as he is concerned.' Then they took off their beautiful dresses, put them away, placed the worn-out shoes under their beds, and lay down.

The next morning the Soldier determined to say nothing, but to see the wonderful doings again. So he went with them the second and third nights. Everything was just the same as the first time, and they danced each time till their shoes were in holes; but the third time the Soldier took away a wine cup as a token.

When the appointed hour came for his answer, he took the three twigs and the cup with him and went before the King. The twelve princesses stood behind the door listening to hear what he would say. When the King put the question, 'Where did my daughters dance their shoes to pieces in the night?' he answered: 'With twelve princes in an

underground castle.' Then he produced the tokens.

The King sent for his daughters and asked them whether the Soldier had spoken the truth. As they saw that they were betrayed, and would gain nothing by lies, they were obliged to admit all. Thereupon the King asked the Soldier which one he would choose as his wife. He answered: 'I am no longer young, give me the eldest.' So the wedding was celebrated that very day, and the kingdom was promised to him on the King's death.

IX

The Mouse, the Bird and the Sausage

ONCE upon a time, a mouse, a bird and a sausage went into partnership; they kept house together long and amicably, and thus had increased their possessions. It was the brd's work to fly to the forest every day and bring back wood. The mouse had to carry water, make up the fire, and set the table, while the sausage did the cooking.

Whoever is too well off is always eager for something new.

One day the bird met a friend, to whom it sang the praises of its comfortable circumstances. But the other bird scolded it, and called it a poor creature who did all the hard work, while the other two had an easy time at home. For when the mouse had made up the fire, and carried the water, she betook herself to her little room to rest till she was called to lay the table. The sausage only had to stay by the hearth and take care that the food was nicely cooked; when it was nearly dinner-time, she passed herself once or twice through the broth and the vegetables, and they were then buttered, salted and flavoured, ready to eat. Then the bird came home, laid his burden aside, and they all sat down to table; and after their meal they slept their fill till morning. It was indeed a delightful life.

Another day the bird, owing to the instigations of his friend, declined to go and fetch any more wood, saying that he had been drudge long enough, and had only been their dupe; they must now make a change and try some other arrangement.

In spite of the fervent entreaties of the mouse and the sausage, the bird got his way. They decided to draw lots, and the lot fell on the sausage, who was to carry the wood; the mouse became cook, and the bird was to fetch water.

What was the result?

The sausage went out into the forest, the bird made up the fire, while the mouse put on the pot and waited alone for the sausage to come home, bringing wood for the next day. But the sausage stayed away so long that the other two suspected something wrong, and the bird flew out to take the air in the hope of meeting her. Not far off

he fell in with a dog, which had met the poor sausage and fallen upon her as lawful prey, seized her and quickly swallowed her.

The bird complained bitterly to the dog of his barefaced robbery, but it was no good; for the dog said he had found forged letters on the sausage, whereby her life was forefeit to him.

The bird took the wood and flew sadly home with it, and related what he had seen and heard. They were much upset, but they determined to do the best they could and stay together. So the bird laid the table, and the mouse prepared their meal. She tried to cook it, and, like the sausage, to dip herself in the vegetables so as to flavour them. But before she got well into the midst of them she came to a standstill, and in the attempt lost her hair, skin and life itself.

When the bird came back and wanted to serve up the meal, there was no cook to be seen. The bird in his agitation threw the wood about, called and searched everywhere, but could not find his cook. Then, owing to his carelessness, the wood caught fire and there was a blaze. The bird hastened to fetch water, but the bucket fell into the well and the bird with it; he could not recover himself and so he was drowned.

X

The Queen Bee

Once upon a time two princes started off in search of adventure, and, falling into a wild, free mode of life, did not come home again.

The third brother, who was called the Blockhead, set out to look for the other two. But when at last he found them, they mocked him for thinking of making his way in the world with his simplicity, while they, who were so much cleverer, could not get on.

They all three went on together till they came to an ant heap. The two elder princes wanted to disturb it, to see how the little ants crept away, carrying their eggs.

But the Blockhead said: 'Leave the little creatures alone; I will not allow you to disturb them.'

Then they went on further till they came to a lake, in which a great many ducks were swimming about. The two wanted to catch and roast a pair.

But the Blockhead would not allow it and said: 'Leave the creatures alone. You shall not kill them.'

At last they came to a bee's nest, containing such a quantity of honey that it flowed round the trunk of the tree.

The two princes wanted to set fire to the tree and suffocate the bees, so as to remove the honey.

But the Blockhead stopped them again and said: 'Leave the creatures alone. I will not let you burn them.'

At last the three brothers came to a castle, where the stables were full of stone horses, but not a soul was to be seen. They went through all the rooms till they came to a door quite at the end, fastened with three bolts. In the middle of the door was a lattice, through which one could see into the room.

There they saw a little grey man sitting at a table. They called to him once – twice – but he did not hear them. Finally, when they had called him the third time, he stood up and opened the door, and came out. He said not a word, but led them to a richly spread table, and when they had eaten and drunk, he took them each to a bedroom.

The next morning the little grey Man came to the eldest prince, beckoned, and led him to a stone tablet whereon were inscribed three tasks by means of which the castle should be freed from enchantment.

This was the first task: In the wood, under the moss, lay the princesses' pearls, a thousand in number. These had all to be found, and if at sunset a single one were missing, the seeker was turned to stone.

The eldest went away, and searched all day, but when evening came, he had only found the first hundred, and it happened as the inscription foretold. He was turned to stone.

The next day the second brother undertook the quest; but he fared no better than the first, for he only found two hundred pearls, and he too was turned to stone.

At last came the Blockhead's turn; he searched in the moss, but the pearls were hard to find, and he got on but slowly.

Then he sat down on a rock and cried, and as he was sitting there, the Ant King, whose life he had saved, came up with five thousand ants, and it was not long before the little creatures had found all the pearls and laid them in a heap.

Now the second task was to get the key of the princesses' room out of the lake.

When the Blockhead came to the lake, the ducks he had once saved, swam up, dived and brought up the key from the depths.

But the third task was the hardest. The Prince had to find out which was the youngest and most charming of the princesses while they were asleep.

They were exactly alike, and could not be distinguished in any way, except that before going to sleep each had eaten a different kind of sweet. The eldest a piece of sugar, the second a little syrup and the third a spoonful of honey.

Then the Queen of the Bees, whom the Blockhead had saved from

burning, came and tried the lips of all three. Finally, she settled on the mouth of the one who had eaten the honey, and so the Prince recognised the right one.

Then the charm was broken, everything in the castle was set free and those who had been turned to stone took human form again.

And the Blockhead married the youngest and sweetest princess, and became king after her father's death, while his two brothers married the other sisters.

XI

The Robber Bridegroom

THERE was once a Miller, who had a beautiful daughter. When she grew up, he wanted to have her married and settled. He thought, *If a suitable bridegroom comes and ask for my daughter, I will give her to him.*

Soon after, a suitor came who appeared to be rich, and as the Miller knew nothing against him he promised his daughter to him. The Maiden, however, did not like him as a bride ought to like her bridegroom; nor had she any faith in him. Whenever she looked at him, or thought about him, a shudder came over her. One day he said to her, 'You are my betrothed, and yet you have never been to see me.'

The Maiden answered: 'I don't even know where your house is.'

Then the Bridegroom said, 'My house is in the depths of the forest.'

She made excuses, and said she could not find the way.

The Bridegroom answered: 'Next Sunday you must come and see me without fail. I have invited some other guests, and, so that you may be able to find the way, I will strew some ashes to guide you.'

When Sunday came, and the Maiden was about to start, she was frightened, though she did not know why. So that she should be sure of finding her way back she filled her pockets with peas and lentils. At the entrance to the forest she found the track of ashes, and followed it; but every step or two she scattered a few peas right and left.

She walked nearly the whole day, right into the midst of the forest, where it was almost dark. Here she saw a solitary house, which she did not like; it was so dark and dismal. She went in, but found nobody, and there was dead silence. Suddenly a voice cried:

Turn back, turn back, thou bonnie Bride,
Nor in this house of death abide.

The Maiden looked up, and saw that the voice came from a bird in a cage hanging on the wall. Once more it made the same cry:

Turn back, turn back, thou bonnie Bride,
Nor in this house of death abide.

The beautiful Bride went from room to room, all over the house, but they were all empty; not a soul was to be seen. At last she reached the cellar, and there she found an old, old woman.

'Can you tell me if my bridegroom lives here?'

'Alas! Poor child,' answered the old woman, 'little dost thou know where thou art; thou art in a murderer's den. Thou thoughtest thou wast about to be married, but death will be thy marriage. See here, I have had to fill this kettle with water, and when they have thee in their power they will kill thee without mercy, cook and eat thee, for they are eaters of human flesh. Unless I take pity on thee and save thee, thou art lost.' Then the old woman led her behind a great cask, where she could not be seen. 'Be as quiet as a mouse,' she said. 'Don't stir, or all will be lost. Tonight, when the murderers are asleep, we will fly. I have long waited for an opportunity.'

Hardly had she said this when the riotous crew came home. They dragged another maiden with them, but as they were quite drunk they paid no attention to her shrieks and lamentations. They gave her wine to drink, three glasses full – red, white and yellow. After she had drunk them she fell down dead. The poor Bride hidden behind the cask was terrified; she trembled and shivered, for she saw plainly to what fate she was destined.

One of the men noticed a gold ring on the little finger of the murdered girl, and as he could not pull it off he took an axe and chopped the finger off; but it sprang up into the air, and fell right into the lap of the Bride behind the cask. The man took a light to look for it, but he could not find it. One of the others said, 'Have you looked behind the big cask?'

But the old woman called out: 'Come and eat, and leave the search till tomorrow; the finger won't run away.'

The murderer said: 'The old woman is right,' and they gave up the search and sat down to supper. But the old woman dropped a sleeping draught into their wine, so they soon lay down, went to sleep and snored lustily.

When the Bride heard them snoring she came out from behind the cask; but she was obliged to step over the sleepers, as they lay in rows upon the floor. She was dreadfully afraid of touching them, but God helped her and she got through without mishap. The old Woman went with her and opened the door, and they hurried away as quickly as they could from this vile den.

All the ashes had been blown away by the wind, but the peas and lentils had taken root and shot up and showed them the way in the moonlight.

They walked the whole night and reached the mill in the morning. The Maiden told her father all that she had been through.

When the day which had been fixed for the wedding came, the Bridegroom appeared, and the Miller invited all his friends and relations. As they sat at table, each one was asked to tell some story. The Bride was very silent, but when it came to her turn and the Bridegroom said, 'Come, my love, have you nothing to say? Pray tell us something,' she answered: 'I will tell you a dream I have had. I was walking alone in a wood, and I came to a solitary house where not a soul was to be seen. A cage was hanging on the wall of one of the rooms, and in it there was a bird which cried:

> Turn back, turn back, thou bonnie Bride,
> Nor in this house of death abide.

'It repeated the same words twice. This was only a dream, my love! I walked through all the rooms, but they were all empty and dismal.

'At last I went down to the cellar, and there sat a very old woman. I asked her. "Does my Bridegroom live here?"

'She answered, "Alas, you poor child, you are in a murderer's den! Your Bridegroom indeed lives here, but he will cut you to pieces, cook you, and eat you." This was only a dream, my love!

'Then the old Woman hid me behind a cask, and hardly had she done so when the murderers came home, dragging a maiden with them. They gave her three kinds of wine to drink – red, white and yellow; and after drinking them she fell down dead. My love, I was only dreaming this!

'Then they took her things off and cut her to pieces. My love, I was only dreaming!

'One of the murderers saw a gold ring on the girl's little finger, and, as he could not pull it off, he chopped off the finger; but the finger bounded into the air, and fell behind the cask on to my lap. Here is the finger with the ring.'

At these words she produced the finger and showed it to the company.

When the Bridegroom heard these words, he turned as pale as ashes, and tried to escape; but the guests seized him and handed him over to justice. And he and all his band were executed for their crimes.

XII

Foundlingbird

THERE was once a forester who went into the woods to hunt, and he heard a cry like that of a little child. He followed the sound, and at last came to a big tree where a tiny child was sitting high up on one of the top branches. The mother had gone to sleep under the tree, and a bird of prey, seeing the child on her lap, had flown down and carried it off in its beak to the top of the tree.

The Forester climbed the tree and brought down the child, thinking to himself, *I will take it home, and bring it up with my own little Lina.*

So he took it home, and the two children were brought up together. The foundling was called Foundlingbird, because it had been found by a bird. Foundlingbird and Lina were so fond of each other that they could not bear to be out of each other's sight.

Now the Forester had an old cook, who one evening took two pails and began carrying water. She did not go once but many times, backwards and forwards to the well.

Lina saw this, and said: 'Dear me, Sanna, why are you carrying so much water?'

'If thou wilt not tell anyone, I will tell thee why.'

Lina said no, she would not tell anyone.

So then the Cook said: 'Tomorrow morning early, when the Forester goes out hunting, I am going to boil the water, and when it bubbles in the kettle, I am going to throw Foundlingbird into it to boil him.'

Next morning the Forester got up very early, and went out hunting, leaving the children still in bed.

Then said Lina to Foundlingbird: 'Never forsake me, and I will never forsake thee.'

And Foundlingbird answered: 'I will never forsake thee.'

Then Lina said: 'I must tell thee now. Old Sanna brought in so many pails of water last night that I asked her what she was doing. She said if I would not tell anybody, she would tell me what it was for. So I promised not to tell anybody, and she said that in the morning, when the father had gone out hunting, she would fill the kettle, and when it was boiling, she would throw thee into it and boil thee. Now we must get up quickly, dress ourselves, and run away.'

So the children got up, dressed quickly, and left the house.

When the water boiled, the Cook went to their bedroom to fetch Foundlingbird to throw him into it. But when she entered the room,

and went up to the bed, both the children were gone. She was terribly frightened and said to herself: 'Whatever am I to say to the Forester when he comes home and finds the children gone? We must hurry after them and get them back.' So the Cook despatched three menservants to catch up the children and bring them back.

The children were sitting near a wood and when they saw the three men a great way off. Lina said to Foundlingbird, 'Do not forsake me, and I will never forsake thee.'

And Foundlingbird answered, 'I will never forsake thee as long as I live.'

Then Lina said, 'Thou must turn into a rosebush, and I will be a rosebud upon it.'

When the three men reached the wood, they found nothing but a rosebush with one rosebud on it; no children were to be seen. They said to each other, 'There is nothing to be done here.' And they went home and told the Cook that they had seen nothing whatever but a rosebush, with one rosebud on it.

The old Cook scolded them, and said: 'You boobies, you ought to have hacked the rosebush to pieces, broken off the bud, and brought it home to me. Off with you at once and do it.' So they had to start off again on the search.

But the children saw them a long way off, and Lina said to Foundlingbird, 'Do not forsake me, and I will never forsake thee.'

Foundlingbird said: 'I will never forsake thee as long as I live.'

Then said Lina: 'Thou must become a church, and I will be the chandelier in it.'

Now when the three men came up they found nothing but a church with a chandelier in it; and they said to each other: 'What are we to do here? We had better go home again.'

When they reached the house, the Cook asked if they had not found anything. They said: 'Nothing but a church with a chandelier in it.'

'You fools,' screamed the Cook, 'why did you not destroy the church and bring me the chandelier?' Then the old Cook put her best foot foremost, and started off with the three men in pursuit of the children.

But the children saw the three men in the distance, and the old Cook waddling behind them. Then said Lina: 'Foundlingbird, do not forsake me, and I will never forsake thee.'

And he said: 'I will never forsake thee as long as I live.'

Lina said: 'Thou must become a pond, and I will be the duck swimming upon it.'

When the Cook reached the pond, she lay down beside it to drink it up, but the duck swam quickly forward, seized her head with his bill and dragged her underwater; so the old witch was drowned.

Then the children went home together as happy as possible, and if they are not dead yet, then they are still alive.

XIII

The King of the Golden Mountain

There was once a merchant who had two children, a boy and a girl. They were both small, and not old enough to run about. He had also two richly laden ships at sea, and just as he was expecting to make a great deal of money from the merchandise, news came that they had both been lost. So now instead of being a rich man he was quite poor and had nothing left but one field near the town.

To turn his thoughts from his misfortune, he went out into this field, and as he was walking up and down a little mannikin suddenly appeared before him and asked why he was so sad. The Merchant said, 'I would tell you at once, if you could help me.'

'Who knows,' answered the little Mannikin. 'Perhaps I could help you.'

Then the Merchant told him that all his wealth had been lost in a wreck, and that now he had nothing left but this field.

'Don't worry yourself,' said the Mannikin. 'If you will promise to bring me in twelve years' time the first thing which rubs against your legs when you go home today, you shall have as much gold as you want.'

The Merchant thought, *What could it be but my dog?* He never thought of his boy, but said 'Yes,' and gave the Mannikin his bond, signed and sealed, and went home.

When he reached the house his little son, who delighted to hold on to the benches and totter towards his father, seized him by the leg to steady himself.

The Merchant was horror-stricken, for his vow came into his head, and now he knew what he had promised to give away. But as he still found no gold in his chests, he thought it must only have been a joke of the Mannikin's. A month later he went up into the loft to gather together some old tin to sell it, and there he found a great heap of gold on the floor. So he was soon up in the world again, bought and sold, became a richer merchant than ever, and was altogether contented.

In the meantime the boy had grown up, and he was both clever and wise. But the nearer the end of the twelve years came, the more sorrowful the Merchant grew; you could even see his misery in his face. One day his son asked him what was the matter, but his father would not tell him. The boy, however, persisted so long that at last he told him that, without knowing what he was doing, he had promised to give him up at the end of twelve years to a little mannikin, in return for a quantity of gold. He had given his hand and seal on it, and the time was now near for him to go.

Then his son said, 'O father, don't be frightened, it will be all right. The little Mannikin has no power over me.'

When the time came, the son asked a blessing of the Priest, and he and his father went to the field together; and the son made a circle within which they took their places.

When the little Mannikin appeared, he said to the father, 'Have you brought what you promised me?'

The man was silent, but his son said, 'What do you want?'

The Mannikin said, 'My business is with your father, and not with you.'

The son answered, 'You deceived and cheated my father. Give me back his bond.'

'Oh, no!' said the little man. 'I won't give up my rights.'

They talked to each other for a long time, and at last they decided that, as the son no longer belonged to his father and declined to belong to his foe, he should get into a boat on a flowing stream, and his father should push it off himself, thus giving him up to the stream.

So the Youth took leave of his father, got into the boat, and his father pushed it off. Then, thinking that his son was lost to him forever, he went home and sorrowed for him. The little boat, however, did not sink. It drifted quietly down the stream, and the Youth sat in it in perfect safety. It drifted for a long time, till at last it stuck fast on an unknown shore. The Youth landed, and seeing a beautiful castle near, walked towards it. As he passed through the doorway, however, a spell fell upon him. He went through all the rooms, but found them empty, till he came to the

very last one, where a serpent lay coiling and uncoiling itself. The serpent was really an enchanted maiden, who was delighted when she saw the Youth, and said, 'Have you come at last, my preserver? I have been waiting twelve years for you. This whole kingdom is bewitched, and you must break the spell.'

'How am I to do that?' he asked.

She said, 'Tonight, twelve men hung with chains will appear, and they will ask what you are doing here. But do not speak a word, whatever they do or say to you. They will torment you, strike and pinch you, but don't say a word. At twelve o'clock they will have to go away. On the second night twelve more will come, and on the third twenty-four. These will cut off your head. But at twelve o'clock their power goes, and if you have borne it, and not spoken a word, I shall be saved. Then I will come to you, and bring a little flask containing the Water of Life, with which I will sprinkle you, and you will be brought to life again, as sound and well as ever you were.'

Then he said, 'I will gladly save you!'

Everything happened just as she had said. The men could not force a word out of him; and on the third night the serpent became a beautiful princess, who brought the Water of Life as she had promised, and restored the Youth to life. Then she fell on his neck and kissed him, and there were great rejoicings all over the castle.

Their marriage was celebrated, and he became King of the Golden Mountain.

They lived happily together, and in course of time a beautiful boy was born to them.

When eight years had passed, the King's heart grew tender within him as he thought of his father, and he wanted to go home to see him. But the Queen did not want him to go. She said, 'I know it will be to my misfortune.' However, he gave her no peace till she agreed to let him go. On his departure she gave him a wishing-ring and said, 'Take this ring, and put it on your finger, and you will at once be at the place where you wish to be. Only, you must promise never to use it to wish me away from here to be with you at your father's.'

He made the promise and put the ring on his finger; he then wished himself before the town where his father lived, and at the same moment found himself at the gate. But the sentry would not let him in because his clothes, though of rich material, were of such strange cut. So he went up a mountain, where a shepherd lived, and, exchanging clothing with him, put on his old smock, and passed into the town unnoticed.

When he reached his father he began making himself known; but his father, never thinking that it was his son, said that it was true he had once had a son, but he had long been dead. But, he added, seeing that he was a poor shepherd, he would give him a plate of food.

The supposed shepherd said to his parents, 'I am indeed your son. Is there no mark on my body by which you may know me?'

His mother said, 'Yes, our son has a strawberry mark under his right arm.'

He pushed up his shirtsleeve, and there was the strawberry mark; so they no longer doubted that he was their son. He told them that he was the King of the Golden Mountain, his wife was a princess, and they had a little son seven years old.

'That can't be true,' said his father. 'You are a fine sort of king to come home in a tattered shepherd's smock.'

His son grew angry, and, without stopping to reflect, turned his ring round and wished his wife and son to appear. In a moment they both stood before him; but his wife did nothing but weep and lament, and said that he had broken his promise, and by so doing had made her very unhappy. He said, 'I have acted incautiously, but from no bad motive,' and he tried to soothe her.

She appeared to be calmed, but really she nourished evil intentions towards him in her heart.

Shortly after, he took her outside the town to the field, and showed her the stream down which he had drifted in the little boat. Then he said, 'I am tired; I want to rest a little.'

So she sat down, and he rested his head upon her lap, and soon fell fast asleep. As soon as he was asleep, she drew the ring from his finger, and drew herself gently away from him, leaving only her slipper behind. Last of all, taking her child in her arms, she wished herself back in her own kingdom. When he woke up, he found himself quite deserted; wife and child were gone, the ring had disappeared from his finger, and only her slipper remained as a token.

'I can certainly never go home to my parents,' he said. 'They would say I was a sorcerer. I must go away and walk till I reach my own kingdom again.'

So he went away, and at last he came to a mountain, where three giants were quarrelling about the division of their father's property. When they saw him passing, they called him up, and said, 'Little people have sharp wits,' and asked him to divide their inheritance for them.

It consisted first of a sword, with which in one's hand, if one said, 'All heads off, mine alone remain,' every head fell to the ground. Secondly, of a mantle, which rendered anyone putting it on invisible. Thirdly, of a pair of boots, which transported the wearer to whatever place he wished.

He said, 'Give me the three articles so that I may see if they are all in good condition.'

So they gave him the mantle, and he at once became invisible. He took his own shape again, and said, 'The mantle is good; now give me the sword.'

But they said, 'No, we can't give you the sword. If you were to say, "All heads off, mine alone remain," all our heads would fall, and yours would be the only one left.'

At last, however, they gave it to him, on condition that he was to try it on a tree. He did as they wished, and the sword went through the tree trunk as if it had been a straw. Then he wanted the boots, but they said, 'No, we won't give them away. If you were to put them on and wish yourself on the top of the mountain, we should be left standing here without anything.'

'No,' said he; 'I won't do that.'

So they gave him the boots, too; but when he had all three he could think of nothing but his wife and child, and said to himself, 'Oh, if only I were on the Golden Mountain again!' and immediately he disappeared from the sight of the giants, and there was an end of their inheritance.

When he approached his castle he heard sounds of music, fiddles and flutes, and shouts of joy. People told him that his wife was celebrating her marriage with another husband. He was filled with rage and said, 'The false creature! She deceived me and deserted me when I was asleep.'

Then he put on his mantle and went to the castle, invisible to all. When he went into the hall, where a great feast was spread with the richest foods and the costliest wines, the guests were joking and laughing while they ate and drank. The Queen sat on her throne in their midst in gorgeous clothing, with the crown on her head. He placed himself behind her, and no one saw him. Whenever the Queen put a piece of meat on her plate, he took it away and ate it, and when her glass was filled he took it away and drank it. Her plate and her glass were constantly refilled, but she never had anything, for it disappeared at once. At last she grew frightened, got up, and went to her room in tears, but he followed her there, too. She said to herself, 'Am I still in the power of the demon? Did my preserver never come?'

He turned to her in anger and said, 'Did your preserver never come? He is with you now, deceiver that you are. Did I deserve such treatment at your hands?' Then he made himself visible and went into the hall, and cried, 'The wedding is stopped, the real King has come.'

The kings, princes and nobles who were present laughed him to scorn. But he only said, 'Will you go, or will you not?' They tried to seize him, but he drew his sword and said: 'All heads off, mine alone remains.'

Then all their heads fell to the ground, and he remained sole King and Lord of the Golden Mountain.

XIV

JORINDA AND JORINGEL

THERE was once an old castle in the middle of a vast thick wood; in it there lived an old woman quite alone, and she was a witch. By day she made herself into a cat or a screech owl, but regularly at night she became a human being again. In this way she was able to decoy wild beasts and birds, which she would kill, and boil or roast. If any man came within a hundred paces of the castle, he was forced to stand still and could not move from the place till she gave the word of release; but if an innocent maiden came within the circle she changed her into a bird, and shut her up in a cage, which she carried into a room in the castle. She must have had seven thousand cages of this kind, containing pretty birds.

Now, there was once a maiden called Jorinda who was more beautiful than all other maidens. She had promised to marry a very handsome youth named Joringel, and it was in the days of their courtship, when they took the greatest joy in being alone together, that one day they wandered out into the forest. 'Take care,' said Joringel, 'do not let us go too near the castle.'

It was a lovely evening. The sunshine glanced between the tree-trunks of the dark green wood, while the turtle doves sang plaintively in the old beech trees. Yet Jorinda sat down in the sunshine, and could not help weeping and bewailing, while Joringel, too, soon became just as mournful. They both felt as miserable as if they had been going to die. Gazing round them, they found they had lost their way and did not know how they should find the path home. Half the sun still appeared above the mountain; half had sunk below. Joringel peered into the bushes and saw the old walls of the castle quite close to them; he was terror-struck, and became pale as death. Jorinda was singing:

My birdie with its ring so red
  Sings sorrow, sorrow, sorrow;
My love will mourn when I am dead,
  Tomorrow, morrow, mor– jug, jug.

Joringel looked at her, but she was changed into a nightingale who sang, 'Jug, jug.'

A screech owl with glowing eyes flew three times round her, and cried three times, 'Shu hu-hu.' Joringel could not stir; he stood like a stone without being able to speak, or cry, or move hand or foot. The sun had now

set; the owl flew into a bush, out of which appeared almost at the same moment a crooked old woman, skinny and yellow; she had big, red eyes and a crooked nose whose tip reached her chin. She mumbled something, caught the nightingale, and carried it away in her hand. Joringel could not say a word nor move from the spot, and the nightingale was gone. At last the old woman came back, and said in a droning voice: 'Greeting to thee, Zachiel! When the moon shines upon the cage, unloose the captive, Zachiel!'

Then Joringel was free. He fell on his knees before the witch, and implored her to give back his Jorinda; but she said he should never have her again, and went away. He pleaded, he wept, he lamented, but all in vain. 'Alas! What is to become of me?' said Joringel. At last he went away, and arrived at a strange village, where he spent a long time as a shepherd. He often wandered round about the castle, but did not go too near it.

At last he dreamt one night that he found a blood-red flower, in the midst of which was a beautiful large pearl. He plucked the flower and took it to the castle. Whatever he touched with it was made free of enchantment. He dreamt, too, that by this means he had found his Jorinda again. In the morning when he awoke he began to search over hill and dale, in the hope of finding a flower like this; he searched till the ninth day, when he found the flower early in the morning. In the middle was a big dewdrop, as big as the finest pearl. This flower he carried day and night, till he reached the castle. He was not held fast as before when he came within the hundred paces of the castle, but walked straight up to the door.

Joringel was filled with joy; he touched the door with the flower, and it flew open. He went in through the court, and listened for the sound of birds. He went on, and found the hall, where the witch was feeding the birds in the seven thousand cages. When she saw Joringel she was angry, very angry – she scolded, and spat poison and gall at him. He paid no attention to her, but turned away and searched among the birdcages. Yes, but there were many hundred nightingales; how was he to find his Jorinda?

While he was looking about in this way he noticed that the old woman was secretly removing a cage with a bird inside, and was making for the door. He sprang swiftly towards her, touched the cage and the witch with the flower, and then she no longer had power to exercise her spells. Jorinda stood there, as beautiful as before, and threw her arms round Joringel's neck. After that he changed all the other birds back into maidens again and went home with Jorinda, and they lived long and happily together.

XV

Clever Elsa

THERE was once a man who had a daughter called Clever Elsa. When she was grown up, her father said: 'We must get her married.'

'Yes,' said her mother, 'if only somebody came who would have her.'

At last a suitor, named Hans, came from a distance. He made an offer for her on condition that she really was as clever as she was said to be.

'Oh!' said her father 'She is as bright as a button.'

And her mother said: 'She can see the wind blowing in the street, and hear the flies coughing.'

'Well,' said Hans, 'if she is not really clever, I won't have her.'

When they were at dinner, her mother said: 'Elsa, go to the cellar and draw some beer.'

Clever Elsa took the jug from the nail on the wall and went to the cellar, clattering the lid as she went, to pass the time. When she reached the cellar she placed a chair near the cask so that she need not hurt her back by stooping. Then she put down the jug before her and turned the tap. And while the beer was running, so as not to be idle, she let her eyes rove all over the place, looking this way and that.

Suddenly she discovered a pickaxe just above her head, which a mason had by chance left hanging among the rafters.

Clever Elsa burst into tears, and said: 'If I marry Hans, and we have a child, when it grows big, and we send it down to draw beer, the pickaxe will fall on its head and kill it.' So there she sat crying and lamenting loudly at the impending mishap.

The others sat upstairs waiting for the beer, but Clever Elsa never came back.

Then the Mistress said to her servant: 'Go down to the cellar, and see why Elsa does not come back.'

The Maid went, and found Elsa sitting by the cask, weeping bitterly. 'Why, Elsa, whatever are you crying for?' she asked.

'Alas!' she answered. 'Have I not cause to cry? If I marry Hans, and we have a child, when he grows big, and we send him down to draw beer, perhaps that pickaxe will fall on his head and kill him.'

Then the Maid said: 'What a Clever Elsa we have;' and she, too, sat down by Elsa, and began to cry over the misfortune.

After a time, as the Maid did not come back, and they were growing very thirsty, the Master said to the Servingman: 'Go down to the cellar and see what has become of Elsa and the Maid.'

The Man went down, and there sat Elsa and the Maid weeping together. So he said: 'What are you crying for?'

'Alas!' said Elsa. 'Have I not enough to cry for? If I marry Hans, and we have a child, and we send it when it is big enough into the cellar to draw beer, the pickaxe will fall on its head and kill it.'

The Man said: 'What a Clever Elsa we have;' and he, too, joined them and howled in company.

The people upstairs waited a long time for the Servingman, but as he did not come back, the Husband said to his Wife: 'Go down to the cellar yourself, and see what has become of Elsa.'

So the Mistress went down and found all three making loud lamentations, and she asked the cause of their grief.

Then Elsa told her that her future child would be killed by the falling of the pickaxe when it was big enough to be sent to draw the beer. Her mother said with the others: 'Did you ever see such a Clever Elsa as we have?'

Her Husband upstairs waited some time, but as his Wife did not return, and his thirst grew greater, he said: 'I must go to the cellar myself to see what has become of Elsa.'

But when he got to the cellar, and found all the others sitting together in tears, caused by the fear that a child which Elsa might one day have, if she married Hans, might be killed by the falling of the pickaxe, when it went to draw beer, he too cried: 'What a Clever Elsa we have!'

Then he, too, sat down and added his lamentations to theirs.

The Bridegroom waited alone upstairs for a long time; then, as nobody came back, he thought: *They must be waiting for me down there, I must go and see what they are doing.*

So down he went, and when he found them all crying and lamenting in a heart-breaking manner, each one louder than the other, he asked: 'What misfortune can possibly have happened?'

'Alas, dear Hans!' said Elsa. 'If we marry and have a child, and we send it to draw beer when it is big enough, it may be killed if that pickaxe left hanging there were to fall on its head. Have we not cause to lament?'

'Well,' said Hans, 'more wits than this I do not need; and as you are such a Clever Elsa I will have you for my wife.'

He took her by the hand, led her upstairs and they celebrated the marriage.

When they had been married for a while, Hans said: 'Wife, I am going to work to earn some money; do you go into the fields and cut the corn, so that we may have some bread.'

'Yes, my dear Hans; I will go at once.'

When Hans had gone out, she made some good broth and took it into the field with her.

When she got there, she said to herself: 'What shall I do, reap first or eat first? I will eat first.'

So she finished up the bowl of broth, which she found very satisfying, so she said again: 'Which shall I do, sleep first or reap first? I will sleep first.' So she lay down among the corn and went to sleep.

Hans had been home a long time, and no Elsa came, so he said: 'What a Clever Elsa I have. She is so industrious, she does not even come home to eat.'

But as she still did not come, and it was getting dusk, Hans went out to see how much corn she had cut. He found that she had not cut any at all, and that she was lying there fast asleep. Hans hurried home to fetch a fowler's net with little bells on it, and this he hung around her without waking her. Then he ran home, shut the house door, and sat down to work.

At last, when it was quite dark, Clever Elsa woke up, and when she got up there was such a jangling, and the bells jingled at every step she took. She was terribly frightened and wondered whether she really was Clever Elsa or not, and said: 'Is it me, or is it not me?'

But she did not know what to answer and stood for a time doubtful. At last she thought: *I will go home and ask if it is me or if it is not me; they will be sure to know.*

She ran to the house, but found the door locked; so she knocked at the window, and cried: 'Hans, is Elsa at home?'

'Yes,' answered Hans, 'she is!'

Then she started and cried: 'Alas! Then it is not me,' and she went to another door; but when the people heard the jingling of the bells, they would not open the door, and nowhere would they take her in.

So she ran away out of the village, and was never seen again.

XVI

Tom Thumb

A POOR peasant sat one evening by his hearth and poked the fire, while his wife sat opposite spinning. He said: 'What a sad thing it is that we have no children; our home is so quiet, while other folk's houses are noisy and cheerful.'

'Yes,' answered his wife, and she sighed. 'Even if it were an only one, and if it were no bigger than my thumb, I should be quite content; we would love it with all our hearts.'

Now, some time after this, she had a little boy who was strong and healthy, but was no bigger than a thumb. Then they said: 'Well, our wish is fulfilled, and, small as he is, we will love him dearly.' And because of his tiny stature they called him Tom Thumb. They let him want for nothing, yet still the child grew no bigger, but remained the same size as when he was born. Still, he looked out on the world with intelligent eyes and

Arthur Rackham

soon showed himself a clever and agile creature, who was lucky in all he attempted.

One day, when the Peasant was preparing to go into the forest to cut wood, he said to himself: 'I wish I had someone to bring the cart after me.'

'Oh, Father!' said Tom Thumb, 'I will soon bring it. You leave it to me; it shall be there at the appointed time.'

Then the Peasant laughed, and said: 'How can that be? You are much too small even to hold the reins.'

'That doesn't matter, if only Mother will harness the horse,' answered Tom. 'I will sit in his ear and tell him where to go.'

'Very well,' said his father, 'we will try it for once.'

When the time came, his mother harnessed the horse, set Tom in his ear, and then the little creature called out 'Gee-up' and 'Whoa' in turn, and directed it where to go. It went quite well, just as though it were being driven by its master; and they went the right way to the wood. Now it happened that while the cart was turning a corner, and Tom was calling to the horse, two strange men appeared on the scene.

'My goodness,' said one, 'what is this? There goes a cart, and a driver is calling to the horse, but there is nothing to be seen.'

'There is something queer about this,' said the other. 'We will follow the cart and see where it stops.'

The cart went on deep into the forest and arrived quite safely at the place where the wood was cut.

When Tom spied his father, he said: 'You see, Father, here I am with the cart; now lift me down.' His father held the horse with his left hand and took his little son out of its ear with the right. Then Tom sat down quite happily on a straw.

When the two strangers noticed him, they did not know what to say for astonishment.

Then one drew the other aside, and said: 'Listen, that little creature might make our fortune if we were to show him in the town for money. We will buy him.'

So they went up to the Peasant and said: 'Sell us the little man; he shall be well looked after with us.'

'No,' said the Peasant; 'he is the delight of my eyes, and I will not sell him for all the gold in the world.'

But Tom Thumb, when he heard the bargain, crept up by the folds of his Father's coat, placed himself on his shoulder and whispered in his ear: 'Father, let me go; I will soon come back again.'

Then his father gave him to the two men for a fine piece of gold.

'Where will you sit?' they asked him.

'Oh, put me on the brim of your hat, then I can walk up and down and observe the neighbourhood without falling down.'

They did as he wished, and when Tom had said goodbye to his father, they went away with him.

They walked on till it was twilight, when the little man said: 'You must lift me down.'

'Stay where you are,' answered the man on whose head he sat.

'No,' said Tom. 'I will come down. Lift me down immediately.'

The Man took off his hat and set the little creature in a field by the wayside. He jumped and crept about for a time, here and there among the sods, then slipped suddenly into a mouse-hole which he had discovered.

'Good evening, gentlemen, just you go home without me,' he called out to them in mockery.

They ran about and poked with sticks into the mouse-hole, but all in vain. Tom crept further and further back, and, as it soon got quite dark, they were forced to go home, full of anger, and with empty purses.

When Tom noticed that they were gone, he crept out of his underground hiding place again. 'It is dangerous walking in this field in the dark,' he said. 'One might easily break one's leg or one's neck.' Luckily, he came to an empty snail shell. 'Thank goodness,' he said; 'I can pass the night in safety here,' and he sat down.

Not long after, just when he was about to go to sleep, he heard two men pass by. One said: 'How shall we set about stealing the rich parson's gold and silver?'

'I can tell you,' interrupted Tom.

'What was that?' said one robber in a fright. 'I heard someone speak.'

They remained standing and listened.

Then Tom spoke again: 'Take me with you and I will help you.'

'Where are you?' they asked.

'Just look on the ground and see where the voice comes from,' he answered.

At last the thieves found him, and lifted him up. 'You little urchin, are *you* going to help us?'

'Yes,' he said. 'I will creep between the iron bars in the Pastor's room and will hand out to you what you want.'

'All right,' they said, 'we will see what you can do.'

When they came to the parsonage, Tom crept into the room, but called out immediately with all his strength to the others: 'Do you want everything that is here?'

The thieves were frightened, and said: 'Do speak softly, and don't wake any one.'

But Tom pretended not to understand, and called out again: 'What do you want? Everything?'

The Maid, who slept above, heard him and sat up in bed and listened. But the thieves were so frightened that they retreated a little way. At last they summoned up courage again, and thought to themselves, *The little rogue wants to tease us*. So they came back and whispered to him: 'Now, do be serious, and hand us out something.'

Then Tom called out again, as loud as he could, 'I will give you everything if only you will hold out your hands.'

The Maid, who was listening intently, heard him quite distinctly, jumped out of bed, and stumbled to the door. The thieves turned and fled, running as though wild huntsmen were after them. But the Maid, seeing nothing, went to get a light. When she came back with it, Tom, without being seen, slipped out into the barn, and the Maid, after she had searched every corner and found nothing, went to bed again, thinking she had been dreaming with her eyes and ears open.

Tom Thumb climbed about in the hay and found a splendid place to sleep. There he determined to rest till day came, and then to go home to his parents. But he had other experiences to go through first. This world is full of trouble and sorrow!

The Maid got up in the grey dawn to feed the cows. First she went into the barn, where she piled up an armful of hay, the very bundle in which poor Tom was asleep. But he slept so soundly that he knew nothing till he was almost in the mouth of the cow, who was eating him up with the hay.

'Heavens!' he said. 'However did I get into this mill?' But he soon saw where he was, and the great thing was to avoid being crushed between the cow's teeth. At last, whether he liked it or not, he had to go down the cow's throat.

'The windows have been forgotten in this house,' he said. 'The sun does not shine into it, and no light has been provided.'

Altogether he was very ill-pleased with his quarters, and, worst of all, more and more hay came in at the door, and the space grew narrower and narrower. At last he called out, in his fear, as loud as he could, 'Don't give me any more food. Don't give me any more food.'

The Maid was just milking the cow, and when she heard the same voice as in the night, without seeing any one, she was frightened, and slipped from her stool and spilt the milk. Then, in the greatest haste, she ran to her master and said: 'Oh, Your Reverence, the cow has spoken!'

'You are mad,' he answered; but he went into the stable himself to see what was happening.

Scarcely had he set foot in the cowshed before Tom began again, 'Don't bring me any more food.'

Then the Pastor was terrified, too, and thought that the cow must be bewitched; so he ordered it to be killed. It was accordingly slaughtered, but the stomach, in which Tom was hidden, was thrown into the manure heap. Tom had the greatest trouble in working his way out. Just as he stuck out his head, a hungry wolf ran by and snapped up the whole stomach with one bite. But still Tom did not lose courage. 'Perhaps the wolf will listen to reason,' he said. So he called out, 'Dear Wolf, I know where you would find a magnificent meal.'

'Where is it to be had?' asked the Wolf.

'Why, in such and such a house,' answered Tom. 'You must squeeze through the grating of the storeroom window, and there you will find cakes, bacon and sausages, as many as you can possibly eat.' And he went on to describe his father's house.

The Wolf did not wait to hear this twice, and at night forced himself in through the grating, and ate to his heart's content. When he was satisfied, he wanted to go away again; but he had grown so fat that he could not get out the same way. Tom had reckoned on this and began to make a great commotion inside the wolf's body, struggling and screaming with all his might.

'Be quiet,' said the wolf. 'You will wake up the people of the house.'

'All very fine,' answered Tom. 'You have eaten your fill, and now I am going to make merry;' and he began to scream again with all his might.

At last his father and mother woke up, ran to the room and looked through the crack of the door. When they saw a wolf, they went away, and the husband fetched his axe, and his wife a scythe.

'You stay behind,' said the man, as they came into the room. 'If my blow does not kill him, you must attack him and rip up his body.'

When Tom Thumb heard his father's voice, he called out: 'Dear Father, I am here, inside the Wolf's body.'

Full of joy, his father cried, 'Heaven be praised! Our dear child is found again,' and he bade his wife throw aside the scythe that it might not injure Tom.

Then he gathered himself together and struck the wolf a blow on the head, so that it fell down lifeless. Then with knives and shears they ripped up the body and took their little boy out.

'Ah,' said his Father, 'what trouble we have been in about you.'

'Yes, Father, I have travelled about the world, and I am thankful to breathe fresh air again.'

'Wherever have you been?' they asked.

'Down a mouse-hole, in a Cow's stomach and in a wolf's maw,' he answered; 'and now I shall stay with you.'

'And we will never sell you again, for all the riches in the world,' they said, kissing and fondling their dear child.

Then they gave him food and drink, and had new clothes made for him, as his own had been spoilt in his travels.

XVII

Sweetheart Roland

ONCE upon a time there was a woman who was a real witch, and she had two daughters; one was ugly and wicked, but she loved her because she was her own daughter. The other was good and lovely, but she hated her for she was only her step-daughter.

Now, this step-daughter had a beautiful apron which the other daughter envied, and she said to her mother that have it she must and would.

'Just wait quietly, my child,' said her mother. 'You shall have it; your step-sister has long deserved death, and tonight, when she is asleep, I will go and chop off her head. Only take care to lie on the further side of the bed, against the wall, and push her well to this side.'

Now, all this would certainly have come to pass if the poor girl had not been standing in a corner and heard what they said. She was not even allowed to go near the door all day, and when bedtime came the Witch's daughter got into bed first, so as to lie at the further side; but when she was asleep the other gently changed places with her and put herself next the wall.

In the middle of the night, the Witch crept up holding an axe in her right hand, while with her left she felt if there was anyone there. Then she seized the axe with both hands, struck – and struck off her own child's head.

When she had gone away, the Maiden got up, and went to the house of her Sweetheart Roland, and knocked at his door. When he came out, she said to him, 'Listen, dear Roland; we must quickly fly. My step-mother tried to kill me, but she hit her own child instead. When day comes, and she sees what she has done, we shall be lost.'

'But,' said Roland, 'you must first steal her magic wand, or we shall not be able to escape if she comes after us.'

The Maiden fetched the magic wand, and then she took her step-sister's head, and dropped three drops of blood from it – one by the bed, one in the kitchen and one on the stairs. After that, she hurried away with her Sweetheart Roland.

When the old Witch got up in the morning, she called her daughter in order to give her the apron, but she did not come. Then she called, 'Where art thou?'

'Here on the stairs,' answered one drop of blood.

The Witch went on to the stairs, but saw nothing, so she called again: 'Where art thou?'

A Rackham

'Here in the kitchen warming myself,' answered the second drop of blood.

The Witch went into the kitchen, but found nothing, then she called again: 'Where art thou?'

'Here in bed, sleeping,' answered the third drop of blood.

So she went into the bedroom, and there she found her own child, whose head she had chopped off herself.

The Witch flew into a violent passion, and sprang out of the window. As she could see for many miles around, she soon discovered her step-daughter hurrying away with Roland.

'That won't be any good,' she cried. 'However far you may go, you won't escape me.'

She put on her seven-league boots, and before long she overtook them. When the Maiden saw her coming, with the magic wand, she changed her Sweetheart into a lake and herself into a duck swimming in it. The Witch stood on the shore, and threw breadcrumbs into the water, and did everything she could think of to entice the duck ashore. But it was all to no purpose, and she was obliged to go back at night without having accomplished her object.

When she had gone away, the Maiden and Roland resumed their own shapes, and they walked the whole night till break of day.

Then the Maiden changed herself into a beautiful rose in the middle of a briar hedge, and Roland into a fiddler. Before long the Witch came

striding along, and said to the fiddler, 'Good Fiddler, may I pick this beautiful Rose?'

'By all means,' he said, 'and I will play to you.'

As she crept into the hedge, in great haste to pick the flower (for she knew well who the flower was), Roland began to play, and she had to dance, whether she liked or not, for it was a magic dance. The quicker he played, the higher she had to jump, and the thorns tore her clothes to ribbons and scratched her till she bled. He would not stop a moment, so she had to dance till she fell down dead.

When the Maiden was freed from the spell, Roland said, 'Now I will go to my father and order the wedding.'

'Then I will stay here in the meantime,' said the Maiden. And so that no one shall recognise me while I am waiting, I will change myself into a common red stone.'

So Roland went away, and the Maiden stayed in the field, as a stone, waiting his return.

But when Roland got home, he fell into the snares of another woman, who made him forget all about his love. The poor Maiden waited a long, long time, but when he did not come back, she became very sad, and changed herself into a flower, and thought, *Somebody at least will tread upon me.*

Now it so happened that a shepherd was watching his sheep in the field and saw the flower, and he picked it because he thought it was so pretty. He took it home and put it carefully away in a chest. From that time forward a wonderful change took place in the Shepherd's hut. When he got up in the morning, all the work was done; the tables and benches were dusted, the fire was lighted and the water was carried in. At dinner-time, when he came home, the table was laid and a well-cooked meal stood ready. He could not imagine how it all came about, for he never saw a creature in his house, and nobody could be hidden in the tiny hut. He was much pleased at being so well served, but at last he got rather frightened, and went to a wise woman to ask her advice. The Wise Woman said, 'There is magic behind it. You must look carefully about the room, early in the morning, and whatever you see, throw a white cloth over it, and the spell will be broken.'

The Shepherd did what she told him, and next morning, just as the day broke, he saw his chest open, and the flower come out. So he sprang up quickly, and threw a white cloth over it. Immediately the spell was broken, and a lovely Maiden stood before him, who confessed that she had been the flower, and it was she who had done all the work of his hut. She also told him her story, and he was so pleased with her that he asked her to marry him.

But she answered: 'No; I want my Sweetheart Roland, and though he has forsaken me, I will always be true to him.'

She promised not to go away, however, but to go on with the housekeeping for the present.

Now the time came for Roland's marriage to be celebrated. According to old custom, a proclamation was made that every maiden in the land should present herself to sing at the marriage in honour of the bridal pair.

When the faithful Maiden heard this, she grew very sad, so sad that she thought her heart would break. She had no wish to go to the marriage, but the others came and fetched her. But each time as her turn came to sing, she slipped behind the others till she was the only one left and she could not help herself.

As soon as she began to sing, and her voice reached Roland's ears, he sprang up and cried, 'That is the true bride, and I will have no other.'

Everything that he had forgotten came back, and his heart was filled with joy. So the faithful Maiden was married to her Sweetheart Roland; all her grief and pain were over, and only happiness lay before her.

XVIII

The Fisherman and His Wife

THERE was once a Fisherman, who lived with his wife in a miserable little hovel close to the sea. He went to fish every day, and he fished and fished, and at last one day, as he was sitting looking deep down into the shining water, he felt something on his line. When he hauled it up there was a great flounder on the end of the line. The flounder said to him, 'Listen, Fisherman, I beg you not to kill me: I am no common flounder, I am an enchanted prince! What good will it do you to kill me? I shan't be good to eat; put me back into the water and leave me to swim about.'

'Ho! Ho!' said the Fisherman. 'You need not make so many words about it. I am quite ready to put back a flounder that can talk.' And so saying, he put back the flounder into the shining water, and it sank down to the bottom, leaving a streak of blood behind it.

Then the Fisherman got up and went back to his wife in the hovel. 'Husband,' she said, 'hast thou caught nothing today?'

'No,' said the Man. 'All I caught was one flounder, and he said he was an enchanted prince, so I let him go swim again.'

'Didst thou not wish for anything then?' asked the Goodwife.

'No,' said the Man. 'What was there to wish for?'

'Alas!' said the Wife. 'Isn't it bad enough always to live in this wretched hovel! Thou mightst at least have wished for a nice clean cottage. Go back and call him, tell him I want a pretty cottage: he will surely give us that.'

'Alas!' said the Man. 'What am I to go back there for?'

'Well,' said the Woman, 'it was thou who didst catch him and let him go again; for certain he will do that for thee. Be off now!'

The Man was still not very willing to go, but he did not want to vex his wife, and at last he went back to the sea.

He found the sea no longer bright and shining, but dull and green. He stood by it and said:

Flounder, Flounder in the sea,
Prythee, hearken unto me:

My Wife, Ilsebil, must have her own will,
And sends me to beg a boon of thee.

The Flounder came swimming up and said, 'Well, what do you want?'

'Alas,' said the Man, 'I had to call you, for my wife said I ought to have wished for something as I caught you. She doesn't want to live in our miserable hovel any longer, she wants a pretty cottage.'

'Go home again then,' said the flounder, 'she has her wish fully.'

The Man went home and found his sife no longer in the old hut, but a pretty little cottage stood in its place, and his sife was sitting on a bench by the door.

She took him by the hand, and said, 'Come and look in here – isn't this much better?'

They went inside and found a pretty sitting room, and a bedroom with a bed in it, a kitchen and a larder furnished with everything of the best in tin and brass and every possible requisite. Outside there was a little yard with chickens and ducks, and a little garden full of vegetables and fruit.

'Look!' said the Woman, 'is this not nice?'

'Yes,' said the Man, 'and so let it remain. We can live here very happily.'

'We will see about that,' said the Woman. With that they ate something and went to bed.

Everything went well for a week or more, and then said the Wife, 'Listen, husband, this cottage is too cramped, and the garden is too small.

The flounder could have given us a bigger house. I want to live in a big stone castle. Go to the flounder, and tell him to give us a castle.'

'Alas, Wife,' said the Man, 'the cottage is good enough for us: what should we do with a castle?'

'Never mind,' said the Wife, 'do thou but go to the flounder, and he will manage it.'

'Nay, Wife,' said the Man, 'the flounder gave us the cottage. I don't want to go back; as likely as not he'll be angry.'

'Go, all the same,' said the Woman. 'He can do it easily enough, and willingly into the bargain. Just go!'

The Man's heart was heavy, and he was very unwilling to go. He said to himself, 'It's not right.' But at last he went.

He found the sea was no longer green; it was still calm, but dark violet and grey. He stood by it and said:

Flounder, Flounder in the sea,
Prythee, hearken unto me:
My Wife, Ilsebil, must have her own will,
And sends me to beg a boon of thee.

'Now, what do you want?' said the flounder.

'Alas,' said the Man, half scared, 'my wife wants a big stone castle.'

'Go home again,' said the flounder, 'she is standing at the door of it.'

Then the man went away thinking he would find no house, but when he got back he found a great stone palace, and his wife standing at the top of the steps, waiting to go in.

She took him by the hand and said, 'Come in with me.'

With that they went in and found a great hall paved with marble slabs, and numbers of servants in attendance, who opened the great doors for them. The walls were hung with beautiful tapestries, and the rooms were furnished with golden chairs and tables, while rich carpets covered the floors, and crystal chandeliers hung from the ceilings. The tables groaned under every kind of delicate food and the most costly wines. Outside the house there was a great courtyard, with stabling for horses, and cows, and many fine carriages. Beyond this there was a great garden filled with the loveliest flowers, and fine fruit trees. There was also a park, half a mile long, and in it were stags and hinds, and hares and everything of the kind one could wish for.

'Now,' said the Woman, 'is not this worth having?'

'Oh, yes,' said the Man; 'and so let it remain. We will live in this beautiful palace and be content.'

'We will think about that,' said the Wife, 'and sleep upon it.'

With that they went to bed.

Next morning the Wife woke up first; day was just dawning, and from her bed she could see the beautiful country around her. Her husband was still asleep, but she pushed him with her elbow, and said, 'Husband, get up and peep out of the window. See here, now, could we not be king over all this land? Go to the flounder. We will be king.'

'Alas, Wife,' said the Man, 'what should we be king for? I don't want to be king.'

'Ah,' said his wife, 'if thou wilt not be king, I will. Go to the flounder. I will be king.'

'Alas, Wife,' said the Man, 'whatever dost thou want to be king for? I don't like to tell him.'

'Why not?' said the Woman. 'Go thou must. I will be king.'

So the Man went; but he was quite sad because his wife would be king.

'It is not right,' he said. 'It is not right.'

When he reached the sea, he found it dark, grey, and rough, and evil smelling. He stood there and said:

Flounder, Flounder in the sea,
Prythee, hearken unto me:
My Wife, Ilsebil, must have her own will,
And sends me to beg a boon of thee.

'Now, what does she want?' said the flounder.

'Alas,' said the Man, 'she wants to be king now.'

'Go back. She is king already,' said the flounder.

So the Man went back, and when he reached the palace he found that it had grown much larger, and a great tower had been added with handsome decorations. There was a sentry at the door, and numbers of soldiers were playing drums and trumpets. As soon as he got inside the palace, he found everything was marble and gold; and the hangings were of velvet, with great golden tassels. The doors of the saloon were thrown wide open, and he saw the whole court assembled. His wife was sitting on a lofty throne of gold and diamonds; she wore a golden crown, and carried in one hand a sceptre of pure gold. On each side of her stood her ladies in a long row, every one a head shorter than the next.

He stood before her, and said: 'Alas, Wife, art thou now king?'

'Yes,' she said; 'now I am king.'

He stood looking at her for some time, and then he said: 'Ah, Wife, it is a fine thing for thee to be king; now we will not wish to be anything more.'

'Nay, Husband,' she answered, quite uneasily; 'I find the time hang very heavy on my hands. I can't bear it any longer. Go back to the flounder. king I am, but I must also be emperor.'

'Alas, Wife,' said the Man, 'why dost thou now want to be emperor?'

'Husband,' she answered, 'go to the flounder. Emperor I will be.'

'Alas, Wife,' said the Man, 'emperor he can't make thee, and I won't ask him. There is only one emperor in the country; and emperor the flounder cannot make thee, that he can't.'

'What?' said the Woman. 'I am king, and thou art but my husband. To him thou must go, and that right quickly. If he can make a king, he can also make an emperor. Emperor I will be, so go quickly.'

He had to go, but he was quite frightened. And as he went, he thought,

This won't end well; Emperor is too shameless. The Flounder will make an end of the whole thing.

With that he came to the sea, but now he found it quite black, and heaving up from below in great waves. It tossed to and fro, and a sharp wind blew over it, and the man trembled. So he stood there, and said:

Flounder, Flounder in the sea,
Prythee, hearken unto me:
My Wife, Ilsebil, must have her own will,
And sends me to beg a boon of thee.

'What does she want now?' said the flounder.

'Alas, flounder,' he said, 'my wife wants to be emperor.'

'Go back,' said the flounder. 'She is emperor.'

So the man went back, and when he got to the door, he found that the whole palace was made of polished marble, with alabaster figures and golden decorations. Soldiers marched up and down before the doors, blowing their trumpets and beating their drums. Inside the palace, counts, barons and dukes walked about as attendants, and they opened to him the doors, which were of pure gold.

He went in, and saw his wife sitting on a huge throne made of solid gold. It was at least two miles high. She had on her head a great golden crown set with diamonds three yards high. In one hand she held the sceptre and in the other the orb of empire. On each side of her stood the gentlemen-at-arms in two rows, each one a little smaller than the other, from giants two miles high down to the tiniest dwarf no bigger than my little finger. She was surrounded by princes and dukes.

Her husband stood still, and said: 'Wife, art thou now Emperor?'

'Yes,' said she. 'Now I am Emperor.'

Then he looked at her for some time, and said: 'Alas, Wife, how much better off art thou for being Emperor?'

'Husband,' she said, 'what art thou standing there for? Now I am Emperor, I mean to be Pope! Go back to the flounder.'

'Alas, Wife,' said the Man, 'what wilt thou not want? Pope thou canst not be. There is only one Pope in Christendom. That's more than the flounder can do.'

'Husband,' she said, 'Pope I will be; so go at once. I must be Pope this very day.'

'No, Wife,' he said, 'I dare not tell him. It's no good; it's too monstrous altogether. The flounder cannot make thee Pope.'

'Husband,' said the Woman, 'don't talk nonsense. If he can make an Emperor, he can make a Pope. Go immediately. I am Emperor, and thou art but my husband, and thou must obey.'

So he was frightened, and went; but he was quite dazed. He shivered and shook, and his knees trembled.

A great wind arose over the land, the clouds flew across the sky, and it grew as dark as night; the leaves fell from the trees, and the water foamed and dashed upon the shore. In the distance the ships were being tossed to and fro on the waves, and he heard them firing signals of distress. There was still a little patch of blue in the sky among the dark clouds, but towards the south they were red and heavy, as in a bad storm. In despair, he stood and said:

Flounder, Flounder in the sea,
Prythee, hearken unto me:
My Wife, Ilsebil, must have her own will,
And sends me to beg a boon of thee.

'Now, what does she want?' said the flounder.

'Alas,' said the Man, 'she wants to be Pope!'

'Go back. Pope she is,' said the flounder.

So back he went, and he found a great church surrounded with palaces. He pressed through the crowd, and inside he found thousands and thousands of lights, and his wife, entirely clad in gold, was sitting on a still higher throne, with three golden crowns upon her head, and she was surrounded with priestly state. On each side of her were two rows of candles, the biggest as thick as a tower, down to the tiniest little taper. Kings and emperors were on their knees before her, kissing her shoe.

'Wife,' said the Man, looking at her, 'art thou now Pope?'

'Yes,' said she. 'Now I am Pope.'

So there he stood gazing at her, and it was like looking at a shining sun.

'Alas, Wife,' he said, 'art thou better off for being Pope?' At first she sat as stiff as a post, without stirring. Then he said: 'Now, Wife, be content with being Pope; higher thou canst not go.'

'I will think about that,' said the Woman, and with that they both went to bed. Still she was not content, and could not sleep for her inordinate

desires. The Man slept well and soundly, for he had walked about a great deal in the day; but his wife could think of nothing but what further grandeur she could demand. When the dawn reddened the sky she raised herself up in bed and looked out of the window, and when she saw the sun rise, she said: 'Ha! Can I not cause the sun and the moon to rise?

Husband!' she cried, digging her elbow into his side. 'Wake up and go to the flounder. I will be Lord of the Universe.'

Her husband, who was still more than half asleep, was so shocked that he fell out of bed. He thought he must have heard wrong. He rubbed his eyes, and said: 'Alas, Wife, what didst thou say?'

'Husband,' she said, 'if I cannot be Lord of the Universe, and cause the sun and moon to set and rise, I shall not be able to bear it. I shall never have another happy moment.'

She looked at him so wildly that it caused a shudder to run through him.

'Alas, Wife,' he said, falling on his knees before her, 'the flounder can't do that. Emperor and Pope he can make, but that is indeed beyond him. I pray thee, control thyself and remain Pope.'

Then she flew into a terrible rage. Her hair stood on end; she kicked him and screamed: 'I won't bear it any longer; wilt thou go!'

Then he pulled on his trousers and tore away like a madman. Such a storm was raging that he could hardly keep his feet: houses and trees quivered and swayed, and mountains trembled, and the rocks rolled into the sea. The sky was pitchy black; it thundered and lightened, and the sea ran in black waves mountains high, crested with white foam. He shrieked out, but could hardly make himself heard:

Flounder, Flounder in the sea,
Prythee, hearken unto me:
My Wife, Ilsebil, must have her own will,

And sends me to beg a boon of thee.

'Now, what does she want?' asked the flounder.

'Alas,' he said, 'she wants to be Lord of the Universe.'

'Now she must go back to her old hovel; and there she is.'

So there they are to this very day.

XIX

The Bremen Town Musicians

ONCE upon a time a man had an Ass, which for many years carried sacks to the mill without tiring. At last, however, its strength was worn out; it was no longer of any use for work. Accordingly, its master began to ponder as to how best to cut down its keep; but the Ass, seeing there was mischief in the air, ran away and started on the road to Bremen; there he thought he could become a town musician.

When he had been travelling a short time, he fell in with a hound, who was lying panting on the road as though he had run himself off his legs.

'Well, what are you panting so for, Growler?' said the Ass.

'Ah,' said the Hound, 'just because I am old, and every day I get weaker, and also because I can no longer keep up with the pack, my master wanted to kill me, so I took my departure. But now, how am I to earn my bread?'

'Do you know what,' said the Ass. 'I am going to Bremen, and shall there become a town musician; come with me and take your part in the music. I shall play the lute, and you shall beat the kettle-drum.'

The Hound agreed, and they went on.

A short time after, they came upon a Cat, sitting in the road, with a face as long as a wet week.

'Well, what has been crossing you, Whiskers?' asked the Ass.

'Who can be cheerful when he is down on his luck,' said the Cat. 'I am getting on in years, and my teeth are blunted and I prefer to sit by the stove and purr instead of hunting round after mice. Just because of this my mistress wanted to drown me. I made myself scarce, but now I don't know where to turn.'

'Come with us to Bremen,' said the Ass. 'You are a great hand at serenading, so you can become a town musician.'

The Cat consented, and joined them.

Next the fugitives passed by a yard where a barn-door fowl was sitting on the door, crowing with all its might.

'You crow so loudly you pierce one through and through,' said the Ass. 'What is the matter?'

'Why! Didn't I prophesy fine weather for Lady Day, when Our Lady washes the Christ Child's little garment and wants to dry it? But, notwithstanding this, because Sunday visitors are coming tomorrow, the Mistress has no pity, and she has ordered the Cook to make me into soup, so I shall have my neck wrung tonight. Now I am crowing with all my might while I have the chance.'

'Come along, Red-comb,' said the Ass; 'you had much better come with us. We are going to Bremen, and you will find a much better fate there. You have a good voice, and when we make music together, there will be quality in it.'

The Cock allowed himself to be persuaded, and they all four went off together. They could not, however, reach the town in one day, and by evening they arrived at a wood, where they determined to spend the night. The Ass and the Hound lay down under a big tree; the Cat and the Cock settled themselves in the branches, the Cock flying right up to the top, which was the safest place for him. Before going to sleep he looked round once more in every direction; suddenly it seemed to him that he saw a light burning in the distance. He called out to his comrades that there must be a house not far off, for he saw a light.

'Very well,' said the Ass, 'let us set out and make our way to it, for the entertainment here is very bad.'

The Hound thought some bones or meat would suit him, too, so they set out in the direction of the light, and soon saw it shining more clearly, and getting bigger and bigger, till they reached a brightly lighted robbers' den. The Ass, being the tallest, approached the window and looked in.

'What do you see, Old Jackass?' asked the Cock.

'What do I see?' answered the Ass. 'Why, a table spread with delicious food and drink, and robbers seated at it enjoying themselves.'

'That would just suit us,' said the Cock.

'Yes; if we were only there,' answered the Ass.

Then the animals took counsel as to how to set about driving the robbers out. At last they hit upon a plan.

The Ass was to take up his position with his forefeet on the windowsill, the Hound was to jump on his back, the Cat to climb up on to the Hound, and last of all the Cock fly up and perch on the Cat's head. When they were thus arranged, at a given signal they all began to perform their music; the Ass brayed, the Hound barked, the Cat mewed and the Cock crowed; then they dashed through the window, shivering the panes.

The robbers jumped up at the terrible noise; they thought nothing less than that a demon was coming in upon them, and fled into the wood in the greatest alarm. Then the four animals sat down to table, and helped themselves according to taste, and ate as though they had been starving for weeks. When they had finished, they extinguished the light, and looked for sleeping places, each one to suit his nature and taste.

The Ass lay down on the manure heap, the Hound behind the door, the Cat on the hearth near the warm ashes and the Cock flew up to the rafters. As they were tired from the long journey, they soon went to sleep.

When midnight was past, and the robbers saw from a distance that the light was no longer burning, and that all seemed quiet, the Chief said: 'We ought not to have been scared by a false alarm,' and ordered one of the robbers to go and examine the house.

Finding all quiet, the messenger went into the kitchen to kindle a light, and taking the Cat's glowing, fiery eyes for live coals, he held a match close to them so as to light it. But the Cat would stand no nonsense; it flew at his face, spat and scratched. He was terribly frightened and ran away.

He tried to get out by the back door, but the Hound, who was lying there, jumped up and bit his leg. As he ran across the manure heap in front of the house, the Ass gave him a good sound kick with his hind legs, while the Cock, who had awoken at the uproar quite fresh and bright, cried out from his perch: 'Cock-a-doodle-doo.' Thereupon the robber ran back as fast as he could to his chief, and said: 'There is a gruesome witch in the house, who breathed on me and scratched me with her long fingers.

Behind the door there stands a man with a knife, who stabbed me; while in the yard lies a black monster, who hit me with a club; and upon the roof the judge is seated, and he called out, "Bring the rogue here," so I hurried away as fast as I could.'

Thenceforward the robbers did not venture again to the house, which, however, pleased the four Bremen musicians so much that they never wished to leave it again.

And he who last told the story has hardly finished speaking yet.

XX

A LONG time ago there was a king who had a lovely pleasure garden round his palace, and in it stood a tree which bore golden apples. When the apples were nearly ripe they were counted, but the very next morning one was missing.

This was reported to the King, and he ordered a watch to be set every night under the tree.

The King had three sons, and he sent the eldest into the garden at nightfall; but by midnight he was overcome with sleep, and in the morning another apple was missing.

On the following night the second son had to keep watch, but he fared no better. When the clock struck twelve, he too was fast asleep, and in the morning another apple was gone.

The turn to watch now came to the third son. He was quite ready, but the King had not much confidence in him and thought that he would accomplish even less than his brothers. At last, however, he gave his permission; so the youth lay down under the tree to watch, determined not to let sleep get mastery over him.

As the clock struck twelve there was a rustling in the air, and by the light of the moon he saw a bird, whose shining feathers were of pure gold. The bird settled on the tree and was just plucking an apple when the young Prince shot an arrow at it. The bird flew away, but the arrow hit its plumage, and one of the golden feathers fell to the ground. The Prince picked it up, and in the morning took it to the King and told him all that he had seen in the night.

The King assembled his council, and everybody declared that a feather like that was worth more than the whole kingdom. 'If the feather is worth so much,' said the King, 'one will not satisfy me; I must and will have the whole bird.'

The eldest, relying on his cleverness, set out in search of the bird, and thought that he would be sure to find it soon.

When he had gone some distance he saw a fox sitting by the edge of a wood; he raised his gun and aimed at it. The fox cried out, 'Do not shoot me, and I will give you some good advice. You are going to look for the Golden Bird; you will come to a village at nightfall, where you will find two inns opposite each other. One of them will be brightly lighted, and there will be noise and revelry going on in it. Be sure you do not choose that one, but go into the other, even if you don't like the look of it so well.'

How can a stupid animal like that give me good advice? thought the King's son, and he pulled the trigger, but missed the fox, who turned tail and made off into the wood.

Thereupon the Prince continued his journey and at nightfall reached the village with the two inns. Singing and dancing were going on in the one, and the other had a poverty-stricken and decayed appearance.

'I should be a fool,' he said, 'if I were to go to that miserable place with this good one so near.'

So he went into the noisy one, and lived there in rioting and revelry, forgetting the bird and all his good counsels.

When some time had passed and the eldest son did not come back, the second prepared to start in quest of the Golden Bird. He met the fox, as the eldest son had done, and it gave him the same good advice, of which he took just as little heed.

He came to the two inns, and saw his brother standing at the window of the one whence sounds of revelry proceeded. He could not withstand his brother's calling, so he went in and gave himself up to a life of pleasure.

Again some time passed, and the King's youngest son wanted to go out to try his luck; but his father would not let him go.

'It is useless,' he said. 'He will be even less able to find the Golden Bird than his brothers, and when any ill luck overtakes him, he will not be able to help himself; he has no backbone.'

But at last, because he gave him no peace, he let him go. The fox again sat at the edge of the wood, begged for its life, and gave its good advice. The Prince was good-natured, and said: 'Be calm, Little Fox, I will do thee no harm.'

'You won't repent it,' answered the fox, 'and so that you may get along faster, come and mount on my tail.'

No sooner had he seated himself than the fox began to run, and away they flew over stock and stone, at such a pace that his hair whistled in the wind.

When they reached the village, the Prince dismounted, and following the good advice of the fox, he went straight to the mean inn without looking about him, and there he passed a peaceful night. In the morning when he went out into the fields, there sat the fox, who said: 'I will now tell you what you must do next. Walk straight on till you come to a castle, in front of which a whole regiment of soldiers is encamped. Don't be afraid of them; they will all be asleep and snoring. Walk through the midst of them straight into the castle, and through all the rooms, and at last you will reach an apartment where the Golden Bird will be hanging in a common wooden cage. A golden cage stands near it for show, but beware! Whatever you do, you must not take the bird out of the wooden cage to put it into the other, or it will be the worse for you.'

After these words the fox again stretched out his tail, the Prince took his seat on it, and away they flew over stock and stone, till his hair whistled in the wind.

When he arrived at the castle, he found everything just as the Fox had said.

The Prince went to the room where the Golden Bird hung in the wooden cage, with a golden cage standing by, and the three golden apples were scattered about the room. He thought it would be absurd to leave the beautiful bird in the common old cage, so he opened the door, caught it, and put it into the golden cage. But as he did it, the bird uttered a piercing shriek. The soldiers woke up, rushed in, and carried him away to prison. Next morning, he was taken before a judge, and, as he confessed all, he was sentenced to death. The King, however, said that he would spare his life on one condition, and this was that he should bring him the Golden Horse, which runs faster than the wind. In addition, he should have the Golden Bird as a reward.

So the Prince set off with many sighs; he was very sad, for where was he to find the Golden Horse?

Then suddenly he saw his old friend the fox sitting on the road. 'Now you see,' said the fox, 'all this has happened because you did not listen to me. All the same, keep up your spirits; I will protect you and tell you how to find the Golden Horse. You must keep straight along the road, and you will come to a palace, in the stable of which stands the Golden Horse. The grooms will be lying round the stable, but they will be fast asleep and snoring, and you can safely lead the horse through them. Only, one thing you must beware of. Put the old saddle of wood and leather upon it, and not the golden one hanging near, or you will rue it.'

Then the fox stretched out his tail, the Prince took his seat, and away they flew over stock and stone, till his hair whistled in the wind.

Everything happened just as the fox had said. The Prince came to the stable where the Golden Horse stood, but when he was about to put the old saddle on its back, he thought, *Such a beautiful animal will be disgraced if I don't put the good saddle upon him, as he deserves.* Hardly had the golden saddle touched the horse than he began neighing loudly. The grooms awoke, seized the Prince, and threw him into a dungeon.

The next morning he was taken before a judge and condemned to deatzh; but the King promised to spare his life, and give him the Golden Horse as well, if he could bring him the beautiful Princess out of the golden palace. With a heavy heart the Prince set out, when to his delight he soon met the faithful Fox.

'I ought to leave you to your fate,' he said. 'But I will have pity on you and once more help you out of your trouble. Your road leads straight to the golden palace. You will reach it in the evening; and at night, when everything is quiet, the beautiful Princess will go to the bathroom to take a bath. As she goes along, spring forward and give her a kiss, and she will follow you. Lead her away with you; only on no account allow her to bid her parents goodbye, or it will go badly with you.'

Again the fox stretched out his tail, the Prince seated himself upon it, and off they flew over stock and stone, till his hair whistled in the wind.

When he got to the palace, it was just as the fox had said. He waited till midnight, and when the whole palace was wrapped in sleep, and the

Maiden went to take a bath, he sprang forward and gave her a kiss. She said she was quite willing to go with him, but she implored him to let her say goodbye to her parents. At first he refused; but as she cried and fell at his feet, at last he gave her leave. Hardly had the Maiden stepped up to her father's bed, when he and every one else in the palace woke up. The Prince was seized, and thrown into prison.

Next morning, the King said to him, 'Your life is forfeited, and it can only be spared if you clear away the mountain in front of my window, which shuts out the view. It must be done in eight days, and if you accomplish the task you shall have my daughter as a reward.'

So the Prince began his labours, and he dug and shovelled without ceasing. On the seventh day, when he saw how little he had done, he became very sad, and gave up all hope. However, in the evening the fox appeared and said, 'You do not deserve any help from me, but lie down and go to sleep; I will do the work.' In the morning when he woke and looked out of the window, the mountain had disappeared.

Overjoyed, the Prince hurried to the King and told him that his condition was fulfilled, and, whether he liked it or not, he must keep his word and give him his daughter.

So they both went away together, and before long the faithful fox joined them.

'You certainly have got the best thing of all,' said he; 'but to the Maiden of the golden palace the Golden Horse belongs.'

'How am I to get it?' asked the Prince.

'Oh! I will tell you that,' answered the fox. 'First take the beautiful Maiden to the King who sent you to the golden palace. There will be great joy when you appear, and they will bring out the Golden Horse to you. Mount it at once, and shake hands with everybody, last of all with the beautiful Maiden; and when you have taken her hand firmly, pull her up beside you with a swing and gallop away. No one will be able to catch you, for the horse goes faster than the wind.'

All this was successfully done, and the Prince carried off the beautiful Maiden on the Golden Horse.

The fox was not far off, and he said to the Prince, 'Now I will help you to get the Golden Bird, too. When you approach the castle where the Golden Bird lives, let the Maiden dismount, and I will take care of her. Then ride with the Golden Horse into the courtyard of the castle; there will be great rejoicing when they see you, and they will bring out the Golden Bird to you. As soon as you have the cage in your hand, gallop back to us and take up the Maiden again.'

When these plans had succeeded, and the Prince was ready to ride on with all his treasures, the fox said to him: 'Now you must reward me for my help.'

'What do you want?' asked the Prince.

'When you reach that wood, shoot me dead and cut off my head and my paws.'

'That would indeed be gratitude!' said the Prince. 'I can't possibly promise to do such a thing.'

The Fox said, 'If you won't do it, I must leave you; but before I go I will give you one more piece of advice. Beware of two things – buy no gallows-birds, and don't sit on the edge of a well.' Saying which, he ran off into the wood.

The Prince thought, *That is a strange animal; what whims he has. Who on earth would want to buy gallows-birds! And the desire to sit on the edge of a well has never yet seized me!*

He rode on with the beautiful Maiden, and the road led him through the village where his two brothers had stayed behind. There was a great hubbub in the village, and when he asked what it was about, he was told that two persons were going to be hanged. When he got nearer, he saw that they were his brothers, who had wasted their possessions and done all sorts of evil deeds. He asked if they could not be set free.

'Yes, if you'll ransom them,' answered the people; 'but why will you throw your money away in buying off such wicked people?'

He did not stop to reflect, however, but paid the ransom for them, and when they were set free they all journeyed on together.

They came to the wood where they had first met the Fox. It was deliciously cool there, while the sun was boiling outside, so the two brothers said, 'Let us sit down here by the well to rest a little and eat and drink.' The Prince agreed, and during the conversation he forgot what he was about, and, never dreaming of any foul play, seated himself on the edge of the well. But his two brothers threw him backwards into it, and went home to their father, taking with them the Maiden, the Horse and the Bird.

'Here we bring you not only the Golden Bird, but the Golden Horse and the Maiden from the golden palace, as our booty.'

Thereupon there was great rejoicing; but the horse would not eat, the bird would not sing and the Maiden sat and wept all day.

The youngest brother had not perished, however. Happily the well was dry, and he fell upon soft moss without taking any harm; only, he could not get out.

Even in this great strait the faithful Fox did not forsake him, but came leaping down and scolded him for not taking his advice. 'I can't leave you to your fate, though; I must help you to get back to the light of day.' He told him to take tight hold of his tail, and then he dragged him up. 'You are not out of every danger even now,' said the Fox. 'Your brothers were not sure of your death, so they have set watchers all over the wood to kill you if they see you.'

A poor old man was sitting by the roadside, and the Prince exchanged clothes with him, and by this means he succeeded in reaching the King's court.

Nobody recognised him, but the bird began to sing, the horse began to eat and the beautiful Maiden left off crying.

In astonishment, the King asked, 'What does all this mean?'

The Maiden answered: 'I do not know; but I was very sad, and now I am happy. It seems to me that my true bridegroom must have come.'

She told the King all that had happened, although the two brothers had threatened her with death if she betrayed anything. The King ordered every person in the palace to be brought before him. Among them came the Prince disguised as an old man in all his rags; but the Maiden knew him at once and fell on his neck. The wicked brothers were seized and put to death; but the Prince was married to the beautiful Maiden and proclaimed heir to the King.

But what became of the poor Fox? Long afterwards, when the Prince went out into the fields one day, he met the fox, who said: 'You have everything that you can desire, but there is no end to my misery. It still lies in your power to release me.' And again he implored the Prince to shoot him dead, and to cut off his head and his paws.

At last the Prince consented to do as he was asked, and no sooner was it done than the Fox was changed into a man; none other than the brother of the beautiful Princess, at last set free from the evil spell which so long had lain upon him.

There was nothing now wanting to their happiness for the rest of their lives.